MW01136149

This book is dedicated to three close and beloved individuals who are no longer with us, and I feel their absence every day. First of all my father, a loving and caring father and grandfather, a noble man, wise and knowledgeable, and at the same time modest and unassuming; and also to my mother, who was his complete opposite – that is, she was a dominant woman, a socialite whose captivating presence could not be ignored, as well as the unique sense of humor which so characterized her. The book is also dedicated to my cousin, Elliel Yossi of blessed memory, a remarkable fighter pilot with an equally remarkable sense of humor. Yossi and I were the same age, and together we shared many unforgettable experiences; he was like a brother to me in every way.

The Red Collusion
David Yaron

Copyright © 2018 David Yaron

All rights reserved; No parts of this book may be reproduced or transmitted in any form or by any means, electronic or mechanical, including photocopying, recording, taping, or by any information retrieval system, without the permission, in writing, of the author.

Contact: dudi.yaron@gmail.com

ISBN 9781792631412

THE
RED
COLLUSION

David Yaron

◆

Moscow, May 1989, Novodevichy Cemetery

THE 500-YEAR OLD NOVODEVICHY CONVENT SITS BY THE
MOSCOW RIVER. It is home to Russia's most revered cemetery.
Some 27,000 sons and daughters of Russia, military heroes
as well as cultural icons, rest in peace completely, some since
the days of Ivan the Terrible. The cemetery's elaborately
decorated tombs, sculpted in stone and granite in the image
of the dead, nestling amidst dense, manicured greenery, lend
it the air of a museum of Russian history. Muscovites enjoy
occasional visits to the Novodevichy Cemetery, as do other
Russians from all over this vast country, who are referred to
condescendingly by the locals as "tourists". Both tourists and
locals follow the custom of leaving colorful bouquets on their
favorite heroes' graves.

Built some eighty years prior to the tumultuous events
of this story, the cemetery reflects the Russian love of order
and discipline. It is divided into sections according to the
deceased's occupation in life, with one area allocated to
writers and others to musicians, playwrights, and masters of
all the arts and sciences.

In the autumn of 1971, Nikita Khrushchev, the Soviet

Union's indisputable leader in the eleven transformative years preceding 1964, was laid to rest in Novodevichy. He was buried secretly, and his death went unreported in the media by order of his successor, Leonid Brezhnev. In fact, the entire cemetery was locked to the public for ten years just to stop his grave from becoming a pilgrimage site for his many admirers.

JUST A FEW STEPS FROM KHRUSHCHEV'S GRAVE, another grave had just been dug, for another great leader of the Soviet Union. The bouquets adorning the fresh grave of Comrade Vladimir Petrovich Yermolov, the General Secretary of the Communist Party of the Soviet Union, were piled so high that they exceeded an average man's height. Thousands of people stood at attention in the cemetery while a small contingent from the Red Army Choir solemnly sang the Anthem of the Soviet Union. It was the revised version, having been rewritten twelve years earlier to eradicate any mention of Joseph Stalin, the ruthless dictator who had led his nation to a costly victory over Nazi Germany. Unlike Stalin, Yermolov had been loved, not feared. The ceremony was broadcast live throughout the eleven time zones of the Soviet Union. On hearing the national anthem, people from all walks of life, throughout the land, stopped their activities and stood in silence in honor of their beloved leader.

When the ceremony was over, the master of ceremonies requested that the crowd remain in place while world leaders left the grounds. As the crowd slowly dispersed, an elderly, slightly bent gentleman leaning on a cane remained in place. Dressed in a gray suit, he raked his fingers through his thin white hair from time to time to protect it from the wind. Beside him stood a young officer dressed in a blue Air Force uniform sporting a shiny golden star insignia set between two blue stripes, indicating his rank of major.

Occasionally, members of the crowd approached the old man, some having a brief word with him.

"Father", said the major to the man by his side, "It seems that even though you left the KGB seven years ago, there are still quite a few people who respect you very much."

The older man smiled wryly.

"I'm not so sure of that, son. They may be expressing their gratitude for my retirement", he suggested, only partly in jest. He took his son's arm. "Let's go now. If we're lucky, we might pass by some of the great sons of our glorious nation."

The two walked slowly from the fresh grave along the high red wall, not unlike the more famous wall of the Kremlin. Here, the less distinguished were interred on four levels resembling miniature Soviet city blocks.

"Father", asked the young man. "Why isn't Secretary Yermolov buried inside the Kremlin, as he deserves? You were very close to him. Was that his wish?"

"Yes, son", replied the aging former chief of the Committee for State Security, otherwise known as the KGB. "It was his specific request when he fell ill. At one of our last meetings, he clearly said that he did not want to become a tourist attraction after his death. Of course he said it with humor – he always had a sense of humor. He wanted to be buried here in Novodevichy, as he did not wish to have politicians as his neighbors. 'They will bore me to death,' he joked. 'I prefer the company of Anton Chekhov, Nikolai Gogol, Sergey Prokofiev.' He may have even mentioned Rostropovich and Shostakovich."

"Was Yermolov fond of classical music, like you?" the

young man wondered.

"Yes, son. He loved good music, just as he loved all the arts. He was especially drawn to writers and playwrights."

The two continued to walk arm in arm on the narrow path along the red wall. They stopped by a tomb bearing the bust of a man holding a violin set atop a tall marble column.

"Father, you seem tired. Do you want to rest for a while?"

"Well, I'm not tired, but the feet... the feet are not what they used to be, you know."

He looked at the bust of the man. "It will be a great honor to rest beside David Oistrakh. He was one of the greatest violinists of the twentieth century. See for yourself – it says so here. He died fifteen years ago."

Nodding, the young man looked down at the marble slab.

"Father, at the funeral today, I heard for the first time that General Secretary Yermolov was also a hero of the Soviet Union. I'm confused. He was not a military man. What did he receive that honor for? And why didn't the public know?"

The retired KGB chief just nodded. "Come, let's go to the gate. Forgive me, son, but this is a long and complicated story in which I too was involved. I'll tell you about it some other time, when the time is right." He looked into his son's eyes.

"Have I disappointed you, son? Let me try to cheer you up with a joke that relates to this situation."

"I'm always happy to hear a good joke", bantered the young man. "Maybe some of the nation's heroes buried around here will enjoy it as well."

"Well", continued the father, "it's a Kazakh story about a father and his son who were leading a camel through the Kazakh desert. They walked for hours without saying a word. At dusk, just before sunset, the father asked the son, 'Why are you quiet son? Why aren't you asking me questions as you always do?' The son answered, 'Why does the sun always rise in the east and set in the west?' The father said, 'I don't know.' Several minutes later the son asked again, 'How can the camel walk for days in the desert without drinking water?' The father again replied, 'I really don't know, son.' The son became discouraged over his father's failure to answer his questions and continued walking in silence. Several minutes later, the father asked his son, 'Why aren't you asking me any more questions? If you don't ask, how will you learn?'" The former KGB chief's son barked a laugh.

"That's a good story. And the moral is clear", he chuckled, patting his father's arm.

"Son", said the former spy chief after walking silently for a while. "No one knows you as well as I do, and I feel you are still disappointed with my answer. But I have an idea.

"It's still early in the afternoon. Let's go sit at the Café Pushkin on Tverskoy Boulevard. Maybe a hot chocolate and vodka will get me to tell you a fascinating story."

And with that, the old man and his young officer son exited the heavy iron gates of the Novodevichy Cemetery and headed for the parking lot.

CHAPTER 1

Moscow, eight years earlier.

Gospodin[1] Vladimir Petrovich Yermolov, or Mister Vladimir, son of Peter, Yermolov, was the way the private secretary of the General Secretary of the Communist Party of the Soviet Union always addressed her superior. In her early forties, Svetlana was tall and pretty, and her lean, upright figure still retained the form of the professional gymnast she had been in her youth. And, like a young athlete, she still kept her chestnut hair pulled back in a bun at the back of her head.

For six years, Vladimir Yermolov had been the General Secretary of the Communist Party, the only party permitted in the Soviet Union. For the past two years, he had also been serving as Chairman of the Council of Ministers, for all intents and purposes acting as both President and Prime Minister. He had become the most powerful man in the Soviet Union.

In 1955, ten years after the war had ended, Yermolov was already a member of the Supreme Soviet, the country's highest legislative body. His analytical skills and attention to detail,

---

1   Literally "lord" in Russian

coupled with his vast knowledge and judicious temper, had earned him the respect of his colleagues.

It was only a few years later that the Supreme Soviet selected Yermolov to serve as the Minister of Industry, a position that accorded him vast powers and authority. He moved quickly to institute industrial reforms; these bore fruit during his term, further increasing his influence and popularity, and thus paving his way to the highest office in the Soviet Union.

The Red Army's commanders never objected to his advance to the top, considering Mr. Yermolov a thoroughly civilian bureaucrat, who lacked military experience even as a soldier; it was inconceivable that he could pose a threat to their authority. His six-year tenure as the party's General Secretary had proved relatively peaceful and uneventful, both domestically and internationally. On the domestic front, thanks to regular rainy seasons, the yields from the wheat crops were sufficient to keep imports of wheat and maize from the United States to a minimum.

Yet his term was far from idyllic. Internationally, the dark clouds of the Cold War were casting their shadow over Soviet-American relations. It was the height of the Cold War, with both nations powerful, armed to the teeth and intent on preserving their interests in the world, not least their prestige. Behind the superpowers' businesslike relations, there were constant conflicts and attempts to supersede each other in various regions worldwide. But Yermolov made sure that very little of the drama was reported and discussed in public. He knew how to keep tensions well under control.

Yermolov, now in his sixties, was quite undistinguished-looking, appearing more like an accountant or a math teacher than a world leader. He was below average height and above average weight. His thinning white hair was always combed to the left. Often, during conferences or conversations, he would pull a small metal comb out of his pocket and run it through his hair. His naturally ruddy complexion was highlighted the red cheeks of a heavy drinker, and the black-rimmed spectacles he always wore sat somewhat sloppily on his nose. Only his family and those few in his inner circle could testify to his biting sense of humor. His forty-year marriage to Irena, a high school teacher, had produced a son, a daughter and three grandchildren. He kept his family away from the limelight, and they were rarely seen or mentioned in the media.

It had been hard for Svetlana to earn the General Secretary's trust, as Yermolov had found in her a serious, irreparable fault: her uncle. Svetlana's mother's brother was Marshal Nikolai Sergeevich Budarenko, Minister of Defense and Executive Commander of the Red Army. Budarenko was, to say the least, a controversial man; hot-tempered and easily provoked to respond loudly and aggressively to any hint of disagreement, which he interpreted as a challenge to his authority. When Yermolov's aides learned of Svetlana's reputation as an excellent office worker who spoke several languages, including English, and was well-versed in arts and letters, they urged him to employ her as his private secretary. Knowing of her family ties to Budarenko, Yermolov was loath to appoint her, but eventually gave in to his aides. Still, even when she did become his private secretary and his closest confidante at work, he ordered the KGB to produce weekly reports on her whereabouts and activities 24 hours a day.

Svetlana was well aware of her boss's suspicious attitude toward her uncle, which bordered on disapproval, and she spared no effort not only to prove her loyalty to her boss, but to ensure that her loyalty was noticed. She had already been his private secretary for two years before Yermolov allowed himself to refer to the Minister of Defense as "your uncle", and even then, not without rancor.

THE GRAND CONFERENCE ROOM IN THE KREMLIN HAD NO windows. Three huge gilt chandeliers, of the same type that adorned the magnificent Mayakovskaya and Taganskaya Metro stations of central Moscow, hung from the lofty, domed ceiling. A massive old oak table, burnished by time, took up most of the room's length, softly reflecting the bright lights from the dozens of electric bulbs in the chandeliers above. Those seated around this table at meetings could imagine that all the sensitive secrets the table had witnessed over the years were concealed under each layer of varnish.

It was early morning, and a small crowd of senior government officials and chiefs of the security services were gathered in their seats around the table. It was too early for a routine meeting, and, indeed, this meeting was an emergency one. At the head of the table, under a huge portrait of Vladimir Ilyich Lenin, founder of the Soviet Union, the General Secretary's seat was empty. The Chief Political Commissar, Sergey Ivanov, was already seated to the right of Yermolov's empty chair. The buzz of conversations held in hushed tones faded to complete silence when the General Secretary appeared in the doorway. All those around the table rose to their feet with respect for their supreme leader.

Yermolov sank into his seat and motioned for everyone to be seated. The topic of this emergency meeting had not been announced, but there was little need for that. All those present knew why they had been invited to this unscheduled meeting.

Everyone waited expectantly for Yermolov to begin, but he took his time. Pulling a white handkerchief out of his pocket, he slowly and methodically cleaned his eyeglasses before placing them back on the bridge of his nose, all the while scanning the faces before him.

"Good morning, Comrades", began the General Secretary, looking intently at each and every participant.

"We met here a week ago. Each of you said what you said and recommended what you recommended, and I was expected to act on your recommendations. I would have acted exactly as you advised me – but I have done just the opposite!" He forcefully banged on the table with his fist, his eyebrows contorted in a scowl and his face becoming redder and redder.

"In Yugoslavia and Romania, the workers' protests have intensified. Worse still, here, at home, we are seeing budding expressions of solidarity with the rebellious reactionary mobs in Yugoslavia and Romania."

The Secretary's eyes were alight with anger.

The KGB chief, Leonid Kliatchko, dressed in the light blue uniform of his office, shifted nervously in his chair. This did not escape Yermolov, who now directed his attention to him.

"I will deal with you soon, Comrade Kliatchko, but right now, just listen to me", Yermolov admonished, pointing a finger at him.

The General Secretary continued, all the while glaring at the KGB chief. "We must operate on two levels simultaneously. First of all, we must personally attack all those individuals abroad who are fomenting trouble and encouraging the traitors in our midst. These people are being organized, financed, and directed by the secret services of the Federal German Republic,

France and the United Kingdom, which all follow the direc-
tives of the Americans and the CIA. As I see it, there is no
difference between intelligence agencies and the governments
that operate them. We will therefore punish these countries.

"Within 24 hours, I want a plan of action from each of you
for undermining the stability and internal security of these
Western states. We operate well-developed KGB infrastructures in all these countries, and we have plenty of *Spetnez*[2]
sleeper fighting cells planted in them. These should be awakened and given a chance to justify their reputations and our
investment. I am not ruling out any means or methods, from
encouraging labor union strikes, to physical sabotage of transportation networks, utility infrastructures and anything else
you may come up with. I want anarchy there! Anarchy – no
less! I want chaos that will ruin the lives of their citizens and
drive them to loathe their own capitalist regimes. We have to
expose these governments' impotence. Is that clear?"

The General Secretary's fist again pounded the table as he
looked for any sign of disagreement among the officials at his
desk.

"I will appropriate any resource that is needed. You can
assume that you have unlimited means from this moment on."

"Is that clear to you?" the secretary was now addressing the
KGB chief.

"This work must be neat. All sabotage in these countries
should be attributed to local organizations and domestic
underground movements. Baader-Meinhof, Red Brigades,
anarchists, whatever. Nothing should point back to us. You
may use your friends from Muslim countries to transport

---

2   Elite KGB units

arms and explosives. This you can do rather well", Yermolov remarked sardonically to his KGB chief.

The General Secretary removed his eyeglasses and rubbed his cheeks.

"And now, to our own internal affairs, and I mean those of our sister states, Yugoslavia, Romania, and especially the German Democratic Republic. Here we need immediate remedial action. We must use our iron fist! In Germany, we will deploy tanks and troops, but carefully, because of the proximity to West Germany which is full of foreign armies. Do you remember Operation Donau in August 1968? Two thousand, not twenty thousand, tanks, were enough to take over all of Czechoslovakia. Do you know why? Because we were creative. We used our brains. We acted wisely", Yermolov expounded, pointing a finger at his temple.

"We sent one hundred of our agents, dressed in civilian clothes, on a commercial flight to Prague International Airport. They seized the airport within minutes and opened it to hundreds of our transport planes, and the rest is history. That is how I want our forces to deal with the GDR; primarily with creativity and logic. If we operate swiftly and forcefully there, eliminating the traitors, the other countries will understand what awaits them. Then you will see all this agitation dying out by itself."

The General Secretary had said enough. He took a break, sipping tea from a glass that had been served to him. He then turned his sharp eyes to Marshal Budarenko, the Minister of Defense.

"Well, Marshal", he said. "I'm sure you have not wasted any time and have already prepared a plan to crush the GDR. We would like to hear it."

Everyone waited for the marshal to speak.

The Defense Minister's oversized military cap, with its huge gold- trimmed visor, lay on the table in front of him. Marshal Nikolai Sergeevich Budarenko, of medium height and with a solid, muscular torso, was well into his sixties and still had the build of a medium- weight boxer. His close-cropped dark hair emphasized his square face and unusually high, protruding cheekbones. His bushy, unkempt brows were already graying. His appearance reflected his character, warning those who crossed his path that his reputation as a tough, opinionated and confrontational man was indeed justified. Few would challenge him in debate or discussion, and none dared to argue with him outright. With one exception – his sole superior, Yermolov.

Budarenko had made a name for himself as a brave in-fantry commander in the Second World War, fighting the Wehrmacht's vastly superior Sixth Army for eight horrific months in Stalingrad. Budarenko, then a lieutenant colonel, was in charge of an ill-equipped unit of tank destroyers. In a series of battles that marked a turning point in the balance of power on the eastern front, Budarenko's poorly-outfitted forces used daring tactics to spread havoc and fear among the German Panzer troops. It was a time of great heroism. The Soviet Union lost more than a million soldiers and Russian civilians in and around Stalingrad. Many more, including Budarenko, were wounded. Although forty years had passed since then, the Defense Minister still had a limp, a souvenir from those terrible days of Stalingrad.

For his courage in Stalingrad, the Marshal had been awarded the prestigious *Medal Za Otvagu*[3]. This medal, made

---

3   Medal of Valor

entirely of silver, featured a silhouette of a T-34 tank and the red Cyrillic letters *Za Otvagu* and *CCCP*, for USSR. Now, as he sat at the conference, the medal, not just the ribbon, was pinned to his jacket, almost lost among the dozens of other medals and ribbons covering the entire front of his army jacket.

The Defense Minister cleared his throat and turned to the increasingly impatient General Secretary.

"Comrade General Secretary Vladimir Petrovich Yermolov", the Defense Minister rasped in a voice roughened by years of heavy smoking. "Regarding the first signs of rebelliousness here at home, I am not at all worried. Comrade Politruk and the Comrade Chief of the KGB know exactly what to do, and they have already informed me of the arrest of seven hundred and fifty hooligans. The main problem, as I see it, is in Western Europe, not in our sister states. All the poison and incitement are coming from these countries. There lies the head of the serpent and there we should hit hard."

The General Secretary leaned back in his seat, expressing no surprise or emotion at what he had just heard, as if to say he had not expected the marshal to propose a worldwide peace initiative.

"Has the Minister finished speaking?" Yermolov asked, somewhat irritably.

"No, Mr. General Secretary", the minister shot back. "I wish to elaborate further. Mr. General Secretary has explained that we occupied Czechoslovakia with two thousand tanks. I was there, commanding an army, and I can tell you that we could have completed the work there in the same time frame even with five hundred tanks. But dealing with NATO is totally different. We will certainly have to deploy a large portion of our armored forces, which we built up precisely for this purpose. I wish to remind you that we have thirty thousand tanks at our disposal. Our numerical advantage over them is so great that we can overwhelm them within three weeks and their regimes will fall like dominos. Even the Americans can't stop us. Their only answer to our massive forces is to deploy tactical nuclear weapons, but they will not dare, because we also have nuclear weapons and it can turn into World War III..."

"What the hell are you talking about, Marshal?" Yermolov snapped, both angry and impatient. "If we invade with thirty thousand tanks, are we not starting a third world war?"

The room fell silent. Yermolov paused, recovered his composure, and said, "What is this, a picnic? A social call? Do you have room on your chest for more medals?"

It was obvious that Yermolov was losing what little patience he had with his Defense Minister.

"I will say this again", Yermolov repeated more calmly, but as authoritatively as ever. "Tomorrow, you, Mr. KGB Chief, will hand me a plan for your operatives' activities inside the western European states.

From you, Marshal, I will receive a plan for a limited entry and takeover of the GDR, that is, East Germany. Do you understand me, Marshal? We are not taking Paris, Rome or London. We are taking Berlin!"

Yermolov stared intensely at Marshal Budarenko, trying to gauge if his message had been received.

"I will be more specific so as to avoid misunderstandings", the General Secretary resumed. "We are aiming for the eastern part of Berlin, the eastern sector only, and even when we get there, we will keep a safe distance from the Berlin Wall."

The General Secretary locked his eyes on both his Defense Minister and the KGB chief. "You two arrange a time with Svetlana to meet me tomorrow. This meeting is closed."

As the General Secretary, followed by his two bodyguards, hurried out of the conference room and back to his office, he was greeted by Svetlana.

"Good morning, Gospodin Vladimir Petrovich Yermolov."

"Good morning, Svetlana", he replied, without slowing his pace. "By the way, regards from your uncle. I so enjoy meeting him, especially early in the morning before the day's work begins."

"Thank you, Sir", Svetlana replied, struggling to hide a grin, as she was well versed in the General Secretary's biting irony. They must have had another shouting match, she thought.

CHAPTER 2

THE GRU SOVIET MILITARY INTELLIGENCE BASE WAS SITU-
ATED IN THE MIDST OF A DENSE FOREST, some twenty miles
outside Moscow. It was a top secret location and very few even
knew of its existence. Sergey Blutin, Marshal Budarenko's loyal aide, had been waiting at the base for two hours, wondering
why he had been summoned there with such great urgency.
The room he was in, with its bare walls and basic function-
al furniture accentuating its gloomy starkness, looked like
a simple, modest classroom. A low wooden platform and a
desk stood at the front of the room near the doorway, with a
green-painted blackboard hanging on the wall behind them.
Three desks and several padded metal chairs occupied the
center of the room.

Every few seconds, Sergey would glance at the five other
men waiting with him. He assumed from their body language
and reticence that, like him, they had just been pulled out
of their regular places of work a short time earlier. He gazed
out of a narrow window at the nearly empty parking lot. He
understood that he had been summoned to discuss a very
sensitive topic, but he struggled to understand the presence of
what looked like a platoon of soldiers in battle gear and carrying assault rifles patrolling the building's grounds. Are they

protecting us from outsiders, or guarding us, he wondered. We are being watched, he concluded, like prisoners. What is going on here, and who are the other five people here, who are probably thinking the same thoughts.

The sound of incoming vehicles cut into his musings, and he returned to his seat at the desk. There was some talk outside before the door opened to usher in the Defense Minister himself. Marshal Budarenko, wearing green army fatigues, strode to the wooden platform and took his seat in front of his small, stunned audience, who stood at attention. The Marshal motioned for them to be seated before pulling a cigarette from a pack of Marlboros and lighting it. He took a deep drag and exhaled the smoke through his nostrils, as if starved for its aroma. He was savoring every moment.

"These Yanks sure know how to make good cigarettes", he joked, trying to lighten the frosty, tense atmosphere in the room. It seemed futile, as his small team of military men sat motionless, seemingly frozen in terror before his intimidating presence.

Another man, wearing a light blue suit, entered the room, carrying a large brown leather case. He approached Budarenko, and, when the Marshal had unlocked the case, ceremoniously pulled out several large sealed manila envelopes and placed them carefully on the Marshal's desk. The Minister of Defense's eyes followed the blue-suited man as he briskly left the room and closed the door.

Marshal Budarenko had not yet finished his cigarette. He scanned the faces of the six silent and expressionless men seated before him, all awaiting a clue from him as to why they were gathered there.

"From now on, until further notice, you are to stay here

in complete isolation and under close surveillance", he finally declared, crushing the cigarette butt in a metal ashtray, never taking his eyes off the six men.

"You will work here, eat here and perhaps even manage to steal a few hours of sleep, also here", he added.

"You are my personal, confidential team of thinkers. Each of you is considered a prodigy in his field. But if any one of you fails to deliver..."

He paused for a moment, raised his right arm, and swiftly sliced the air in a beheading motion. There was no need for further explanation.

"Am I clear? If any one of you fails, he will be replaced immediately with another, most talented man. Your replacements are ready – there is another team of six here on base, and any one of them can replace each and every one, or all of you, at a moment's notice."

His audience remained rigid with fright. The atmosphere was grim. Marshal Budarenko was most certainly living up to his reputation.

"Each of you will receive one of these sealed envelopes with an order personally signed by me. It is intended for anyone in the Soviet Union who can help you acquire anything you need to complete your mission, including arms, equipment and personnel. They are ordered to fulfill your request immediately, regardless of their rank or status or whether they are military or civilian. All possible means are at your disposal, including any transportation to any destination, by land, sea or air.

"And remember, you are not alone here. You will remain here 24 hours a day under surveillance. Your liaison officer with me is the civilian gentleman who entered this room a few minutes ago. You will direct any questions or requests to him."

The six men remained silent. They still had no clue as to their mission, and none dared to ask. What was certain was that their lives were changing before their eyes.

"Sergey, we'll start with you", announced the marshal.

Sergey, who up until a few hours before had been working as a senior aide to the Minister, stood up. His soon-to-be colleagues did not yet know who he was.

"Yes, Mr. Minister", he responded.

"You, Sergey, have an easy task, which you will complete before morning. You will prepare a detailed, comprehensive paper for me to submit to Comrade General Secretary. In this document, which I will personally present to Mr. General Secretary for his approval, you will detail and explain the methods of action and orders of battle sufficient to invade and seize control of the German Democratic Republic as swiftly as possible. You will leave no question unanswered. I want the order of battle to be as large as possible, much larger than we need just for this mission. I trust you will find justifications, such as the harsh winter and the mud that will slow the progress of our armored columns, as well as other possible reasons, so long as they seem rational and proportional. But that is not all. I also want you to prepare a Phase B plan for me, in which I want a full outline for deploying as many of our armored forces as possible as a reserve, at a reasonable distance from the border between the two German republics. These, even if stationed outside the GDR, should be able to cross into West Germany within 36 to 48 hours of receiving their orders. This reserve, or maybe even the main force, should be able to leverage the advantages gained by Phase A's invading force and enter West Germany by surprise, thereby expanding and deepening our hold of the NATO territory that we will then occupy.

"Do you understand your mission, Sergey?" the Minister of Defense barked.

"Yes, Mr. Minister. It is clear to me."

Marshal Budarenko lit another cigarette and, flabbergasting his new team with a most uncharacteristic act, pushed the pack of cigarettes to the end of the table towards his men.

"If any of you wants to smoke a good American cigarette, be my guest", he offered.

This gesture was entirely out of character for Marshal Budarenko, who was, after all, a high-ranking bully who treated his men as formally and harshly as was possible. Perhaps he was indeed wooing them?

Of course, not one of the men dared to even think of smoking the marshal's prized cigarettes.

Budarenko reached out and collected the pack quickly enough, placing it close to him where it had been. "Now we come to the real matter", he revealed.

"Our beloved Soviet Union is in existential danger. You are the few, the best men, selected for this historic mission of saving our motherland from harm. Even if we suppress the stubborn rebellion in the GDR, not only will we not have eliminated rebellions in other countries, but this may even breathe new life into these reactionary insurgencies. If this happens, the small pockets of discontent we are already witnessing here at home will grow, intensify, spread, and eventually threaten the very existence of the Soviet Union. Every one of you knows that our country is composed of dozens of different nationalities, many with different cultures, faiths and languages, some even dreaming of independence.

"If the rebels in Yugoslavia, Romania and the GDR manage to mobilize the masses and depose the communist regimes in their states, there will be a massive snowball effect that will erupt into our own country. I do not want to think what could happen if the Ukrainian people suddenly decided to break away from us. The Ukrainians sit on the Black Sea, home to our Black Sea Fleet, armed with great quantities of nuclear weapons to deter our enemies. Do you understand? You are being entrusted with the great historic privilege of saving our motherland."

The six men exchanged glances, trying to assess each other's reaction to the Minister's words.

"No one in the Kremlin understands this as fully as I do. They do not know what is required to defend the motherland!"

The Minister spoke with great passion, raising his voice as if addressing a massive audience.

"Our operation in the GDR will benefit us there, but it will not remove the threat to our union, and as I said, it might even escalate the situation. It all begins and ends with the belligerent western European states of NATO. They incite all the unrest. They finance the troublemakers and direct them from there. Eventually, the cure for this disease must be administered there. Only by striking these countries good and hard will we eliminate the danger. And when we fight against an outside enemy, all Soviet citizens stand united behind the Red Army.

"And now to the mission before you."

The Marshal's ashtray was filling up with cigarette butts, and the room became smokier as he spoke.

"Our forces will deploy to the west of the Soviet Union within days, and will be positioned within striking distance of Western Europe. However, in order to actually strike and invade, we must first create a reason, a cause to justify our actions. If we hit them first, we are bullies, but if we let them hit us first, we will be acting in self-defense. We need to create an incident serious enough to warrant such an operation, and you will be the ones to create it. As I said before, out of all the sons of the Soviet Union, you were selected for this mission. You will submit a plan to generate an event that will make our invasion of the West seem a legitimate and justified retaliatory action.

"Each of you was vetted not just for skill and creativity but also for background. We checked your family histories back to your great- grandparents. Your loyalty, to the country and to the party, and that of your families and friends, have been proven beyond a doubt. You will provide me with the plan I need, even if it entails a substantial sacrifice of Soviet citizens."

The Minister of Defense completed his speech and lit yet another cigarette. Leaning back in his seat, he placed his enormous palms on his desk.

"Is everything clear?"

"Mr. Minister of Defense", someone from the team ventured. Everyone turned to identify the man with the courage to address the Marshal without first asking for permission. The Minister addressed the team member by name and rank.

"Yes, Colonel Yevgeni, speak up."

Colonel Yevgeni rose to his feet. On the short side, very thin and hunched, and wearing thick eyeglasses, he did not look like a military man. His colleagues and the Marshal were anxious to hear what he had to say.

"Comrade Marshal, Minister of Defense, you may not have explicitly stated the nature of the event to be planned, but as a mathematician and physicist, I deal with formulas and unknowns. All the required components you mentioned make sense in only one context, and, in combination, lead to one conclusion that is quite clear. Only an offensive by hostile powers can pave the way for us to embark on an extensive retaliatory action in Western Europe. We must cause a sufficiently cataclysmic event - for example, a nuclear incident within Soviet territory - that can be blamed on American aggression. Do I understand your intention correctly, Mr. Minister?"

Absolute silence descended on the room. The Colonel's five colleagues were nervous, each squirming uncomfortably in fear of the Marshal's reaction. It was obvious that what the Colonel had suggested bordered on the unthinkable, if not the insane. But everything depended on the response this idea would elicit from the Minister of Defense. They could either admire Colonel Yevgeni for his courage, or pity him for his stupidity. Everything depended on the man at the head of the table.

To their amazement, the Minister of Defense nodded approvingly at the Colonel.

"Now you understand why we chose you for this mission", the Minister acknowledged. "You could not have expressed it better or more clearly. You grasped what I want to achieve and were able to fathom what I meant. However, I expect you to create a situation that is not the real thing but only looks like the real thing, simulating the effects of such a catastrophe but without all the destructive consequences. If you can do this, we will save human lives. However, I am afraid that this may be impossible. Even my advisers are skeptical, claiming that in the real world, one can either be pregnant or not pregnant – one cannot be half pregnant."

The Minister got up just as the mysterious civilian in the light blue suit suddenly re-entered the room.

"This is Gregory", the minister explained. "From now on, he is your father and mother, your wife and your mistress. He has direct access to me twenty-four hours a day, seven days a week. I want to hear ideas by tomorrow. Good luck."

The Minister walked to the door and Gregory followed him, hurrying to match his pace. The six teammates were all alone now, trying to come to terms with the complex and sensitive situation they now found themselves in. The Marshal had not introduced them to each other, and none of them felt comfortable enough to start a conversation yet. The six were partners in destiny. They continued to disregard each other's presence, but not for long.

Marshal Budarenko's convoy of official black cars entered the Kremlin gates. Svetlana greeted her uncle formally and ushered him into the General Secretary's office. His bodyguards remained in the reception area, which was Svetlana's domain.

Budarenko took his seat at the General Secretary's desk. Yermolov cleared his throat and looked at his Defense Minister expectantly while sipping his tea. The minister removed from his case a thin folder with two thick red lines across one corner and the words TOP SECRET stamped on it in large red letters.

The minster placed the folder in front of Yermolov, who glanced at it for a moment before turning to the Defense Minister.

"What have you brought me this morning?" Yermolov inquired.

"This, Mr. General Secretary, is the plan for the introduction of forces into the German Democratic Republic", replied the minister.

"Good. And what order of battle do you require to restore order there?" asked the General Secretary.

"In the first phase, ten thousand tanks, plus reserve forces near the border."

The General Secretary could not believe his ears. He stood up, still clutching his steaming cup of tea. His whole body shook. He put his cup on the desk and stared straight into the eyes of his Minister of Defense.

"Ten thousand tanks", he roared. "Now tell me, Mr. Minister, are you confused with the zeros? I think I heard one more zero than needed. You meant one thousand tanks, didn't you? Only yesterday you said that in 1968, in Czechoslovakia, you could have succeeded with only five hundred tanks. Now you need twenty times more? Why? Both countries are similar in size and population. Why do you need all this force?"

Marshal Budarenko did not respond.

"Do you want all of NATO to be on red alert?" continued the General Secretary in a raised voice. "I don't understand you, I really don't, Why does everything you do have to be grand, bombastic?"

"Mr. General Secretary", Marshal Budarenko replied, "If you read the whole document in front of you, you will find all the answers to your questions. But to address your question about Czechoslovakia, there are substantial differences between the situations in the two countries. In Czechoslovakia, we acted in summer, in August, and now, in the GDR, it is winter. Germany is much further north than Czechoslovakia, and its winter is harsher, wetter and muddier. Our tanks will be less mobile. Therefore, we will need many, many more tanks as backup."

"Mr. Marshal", the General Secretary reverted to the form

of address he often used when at odds with his minister. "I am not an expert like you in maneuvering armored columns, but if the surface is impassable to one tank, then it is impassable to ten and even one thousand tanks. If you have any doubts about the tanks' abilities to manouver, send fewer tanks and more armored personnel carriers that are lighter and more mobile."

He paused, expecting an answer from the Minister, but this did not come. "Why do we need all these tanks? Who do you think you'll be fighting there? These are civilians, workers and students."

The rivalry between these two men, close in age and with similar backgrounds in the Great Patriotic War, as WWII was known in the Soviet Union, was long-standing. Yet Marshal Budarenko knew that he could not deceive his superior as he had deceived others. Now he could not help but admire the "civilian", as he derisively called the General Secretary behind his back, especially in closed military meetings. He recognized Yermolov's outstanding analytical abilities and common sense, and he was thankful for Yevgeni's superior planning talent to help him clear the hurdles facing him.

"Mr. General Secretary", the minister repeated calmly. "All the answers to your questions are here, in this document that I gave you. But I would say that my mission and duty are to prepare our Armed forces to face the worst scenario. The rebels' strength and influence are so great now that it is possible, even probable, that in response to our invasion, the German Democratic leadership will order the *Landstreitkraft*[4] to resist us and fight on the side of the rebels. I must remind

---

4   The GDR's land forces

you, Mr. Secretary, that the GDR has the second strongest army among our Warsaw Pact allies. We were quick and eager to supply them with every modern tank that we produced. They are equivalent to us in the quality of their ordinance. As I see it, it is highly likely that we will find them facing us and defending their land against our forces. Therefore, we must have an overwhelming force, to suppress any notion they might have of resisting us."

General Secretary Yermolov was beginning to feel that he had reached an impasse. In the past, the Marshal, with characteristic hardheadedness, had dug in and refused to reconsider his position, and he was likely to do so now. He is not about to downsize the force, definitely not the number of tanks, the General Secretary thought. Several minutes later, Yermolov signed Marshal Budarenko's invasion plans. At least the Defense Minister had conceded, or so Yermolov rationalized, by not planning to invade Western Europe and start another great war. Let the minister have something, rather than everything or nothing at all, Yermolov reasoned.

Marshal Budarenko left the General Secretary's office in much higher spirits than when he had entered. He smiled at Svetlana with a half wink as he exited her reception area. He had good reason to be satisfied, having gained the General Secretary's approval of his plan to amass the most powerful armored forces ever assembled in modern history just a few hundred miles from his greatest enemy, the Federal Republic of Germany. Yermolov's approval guaranteed the Politburo's approval as well. In time, Budarenko would also mobilize the reserve forces. Soon he would be commanding the largest armored forces the world had ever known.

CHAPTER 3

THE SIX MEMBERS OF THE THINK TANK HAD SPENT SOME time together, although *together* was true only as far as their being in the same room. They sat at their desks with their documents and writing paper before them. They were working under tremendous strain. Their short deadline and the magnitude of the mission, not least its utmost importance for the future security of their country, inhibited them from producing the brightest, most daring ideas that they could have had under better circumstances. As though the pressure to excel was not enough, their personal careers were also on the line. Marshal Budarenko's words of "encouragement" still echoed in their minds. One could easily be transferred to a job in much colder, more desolate environments. For hours, they had not raised their voices above a whisper.

The intrepid Colonel Yevgeni was focused on a pile of papers strewn on the desk. From time to time, he would lean towards a man with cropped hair sitting to his right, whom he always addressed by his military rank, Brigadier General Dimitri. The two would exchange information and ideas while jotting down short notes.

The other four team members sat nearby in silence, occasionally glancing at the two working beside them. It seemed that the crew had decided to let Marshal Budarenko's burden rest on the thin shoulders of Colonel Yevgeni and the broader ones of Brigadier General Dimitri.

Suddenly the door opened, squeaking on its rusty hinges, and in came Gregory in his light blue suit. "Mr. Defense Minister has arrived", he announced, and the six men rose to attention.

The Minister entered briskly, as usual. To everyone's surprise, he grabbed a chair and joined them at their desk.

"Good morning, officers", Budarenko greeted them. He was in a much better mood than the day before.

"Good morning, Mr. Minister of Defense", the six replied almost in unison.

The minister turned to Sergey. "Sergey", he said, "The operation order that you prepared for me yesterday has already been signed by Mr. General Secretary. What have you prepared for me now?"

Although the question was directed at all the team members, it was obvious to everyone that Colonel Yevgeni would answer. He and Dimitri had been working on a joint plan, and Yevgeni, although lower in rand than the Brigadier General, had the ear of the Defense Minister.

But it was Dimitri who rose to his feet, tapping Yevgeni's shoulder as if to say, "Leave this to me. I know how to handle the Marshal." He looked directly at Defense Minister Budarenko.

Brigadier General Dimitri was the epitome of the fit, active Soviet junior general. His jet black hair was thick and precisely cropped. A handsome man of average height, his physique was athletic and he walked with a springy gait. The beige turtleneck sweater he wore indicated his branch of service –

the Navy. He had only recently received his rank of Brigadier General, after being transferred from his long service in the navy to general military intelligence.

Marshal Budarenko pointed at him like a schoolteacher. "Brigadier

General Dimitri, speak!"

"Mr. Minister", began Dimitri. "We have so far conducted a preliminary examination of two options. One we have already deemed too difficult to execute. The second, we need to test in the field."

Dimitri paused, looking nervously at the minister.

"Go on. I'm listening", coaxed the marshal.

"We've checked how a ballistic missile is launched from an American submarine. Namely, the chain of command to approve such a launch and whether the missile can be aimed at a specific target that is less sensitive, from our point of view, or whether the target is pre- programmed and locked into the missile's navigation system."

The Brigadier General paused, waiting for the Minister to respond, but the Minister motioned to him to continue.

"We've checked with naval intelligence here, and with our KGB people in Washington. The Americans' most advanced submarine is operated by a crew of 15 officers and 140 men. As the Americans have 91 such submarines, their total submarine force is 14,000 seamen and officers.

"We requested information from our Washington staff and, just as we thought, they have good intelligence and real-time data on some of the officers and seamen in the submarine fleet. We checked the feasibility of bribing or using some means of coercion to compel some crew members to cooperate with us and launch a missile. It quickly became obvious that this course would be complicated, even impossible, as both the submarine captain and the first officer wear the keys to the safe box, where the launch codes are stored, around their necks 24 hours a day. The safe box can only be opened with both keys simultaneously. Because we concluded that this option requires a hostile action and a violent takeover of the vessel, we rejected it."

Beginning to lose his patience, Marshal Budarenko was about to erupt at any moment. He hated being told what could not be done, especially in detail. He glanced at his watch.

"Good, Brigadier General", he said. "Now that I know what is not possible, could you kindly tell me what is possible and how it can be done?"

Dimitri was taken aback, but soon recovered, and continued his presentation in an even voice.

"We continued our inquiry. If not the Navy, then the Army, the tactical field units, where we assume the procedures and rules of engagement are not as strict."

"What do you mean by tactical units, Brigadier General?" Marshal Budarenko interrupted.

"I mean the Pershing missile batteries deployed in West Germany. These are relatively small missiles placed on mobile platforms, not in underground fortified bunkers. They are very much like our own SS-20 missile batteries, except that the Pershing is even lighter and more mobile."

"I know the Pershing", the Marshal snapped. "Go on, Dimitri."

"Using the Pershing, a violent takeover could be successful, although it could leave traces. But we have found a better option.

"I spoke with our staff in the Federal Republic last night, and received some useful intelligence from them. The American soldiers manning the Pershing batteries are not as disciplined as the ones in the submarine fleet. They are bored. They leave their bases in the evenings and go out drinking, passing their time in bars and discotheques in the surrounding towns. Our men, and especially our women, know what to do with them. They have marked several men who can be captured, isolated and interrogated to tell us how their batteries function up to the stage of pressing the launch button."

"Very well", interjected Marshal Budarenko, lighting a cigarette. "This is getting interesting, but hurry up. Our time is short."

"Our most qualified personnel in this matter are stationed in the Cologne area", Dimitri explained. "A Pershing battery is deployed near a small town east of Cologne, called Siegen, in an isolated and mountainous area. Our people recommend that we concentrate on this battery. They even say they can bring one of its senior operators here."

"Bring him here? No!" countered Budarenko. "You go there yourself and squeeze all the information you need from that operator. Then, based on this information, you will decide if we can take over the battery and execute a launch, or convince the American to perform the launch himself. I know that our people there have the means to get people to do things."

Marshal Budarenko now turned to Gregory, sitting to his right, who had not spoken since entering. Budarenko pointed at Dimitri.

"Gregory, prepare a west European passport for Dimitri. I see no reason why he cannot leave within two hours, to … Bieden? What's the name of the town again?"

"Siegen, Mr. Minister of Defense", said Dimitri.

"All right, Siegen", repeated Marshal Budarenko. "Is that

clear, Gregory?"

Gregory rose to his feet. "Yes, Minister. Dimitri will be there within a few hours."

Marshal Budarenko folded his arms on his chest. "I am not pleased that you have presented me with only one plan so far. If Brigadier General Dimitri returns with answers that rule out the Pershing option, then what? We start again? I want you to use this time until Dimitri returns to create even smarter alternatives that may be easier and safer to execute. Is this clear?"

"Yes, Mr. Minister", the team members chorused.

All the officers rose to their feet when the marshal stood and walked out the door, followed by Gregory. There was relief at his exit, and Dimitri's five colleagues looked at him with appreciation. Would he be the one to come up with a winning plan that would relieve them of the burden of satisfying Marshal Budarenko's whims?

A uniformed soldier entered the room and instructed Dimitri to follow him outside.

THE WHEELS OF THE AEROFLOT TUPOLEV 154 AIRLINER had just detached from the concrete runway at Moscow's Domodedovo Airport. The plane shot up to the skies with a deafening noise while banking right in a wide circle to the west. Within four hours, it would land at Geneva International Airport in Switzerland.

Brigadier General Dimitri scanned the faces of the passengers on the plane, which was largely empty; only about a third of the seats were taken. How many of these passengers were heading for a ski vacation in the Alps, he wondered. Probably none. He speculated as to how many of the passengers were on a state mission. He recognized none of the faces.

I must try to remember each and every face, he thought. One of them must be following me, and he or she will probably board the connecting flight to Germany as well. He reclined his seat, let go of his thoughts and was soon fast asleep. He had not slept for 36 hours.

Three hours later, he was already seated in a Lufthansa Boeing 727 for the short flight to Cologne's Bonn Airport. This flight was to last less than an hour, and Dimitri unbuckled his seat belt and walked to the restroom in the back of the plane, all the while scanning the faces of each passenger. He could not recognize any from his earlier flight from Moscow. But when he returned to his seat, he could not help noticing the face of a woman in her thirties. There was nothing distinctive about her features, and when he returned to his seat, he wondered why she, of all people on the plane, had attracted his attention.

Then he smiled faintly with a sense of victory. His instincts had not failed him this time, as they had too many other times before. It was the same young woman who had traveled on the plane with him from Moscow, except that now she had combed her hair back into a pony tail and changed from a red dress into a green one, probably at the airport in Geneva. He had no doubt that she was the same woman. It was an amusing game, he thought, when the one followed always knew he was being followed, and the only question was by whom. If my colleagues do not pick me up in Cologne, he thought, I could at least ask her to give me a ride to the city.

Dimitri made a mental note that upon his return to Moscow, he should tell Gregory to make sure that the next time, the woman should wear something less conspicuous and flashy.

The landing at Cologne's Bonn airport was rough and

accompanied by loud scraping noises when the landing gear hit the tarmac. In the shuttle transporting the passengers to the terminal, Dimitri again noticed the woman in green as she stood just a few meters away with her back to him. Within five minutes he was already at passport control, this time as James Andrew Miller, a British citizen. The fake British passport looked authentic, yet there was no escaping his anxiety as the German immigration officer leafed through its pages.

"Business or tourist?" he asked. "Tourist."

The officer quickly stamped the passport and handed it back to Dimitri, who walked briskly through the luggage area outside to a cold, overcast early evening.

"Mr. Miller?" a tall, blond man in a tailored suit and tie stood before him, a black coat over his arm.

"Yes, that's me", Dimitri replied.

"My name is Wolfgang. I'm pleased to meet you", said the blond man in perfect German. "Please follow me."

The two walked away from the terminal to the parking lot. Wolfgang opened the rear right door of a black Mercedes with its engine running.

Dimitri sank into the black leather seat and Wolfgang joined him on the other side. The driver, a huge man, seemed to be sitting in a tiny seat, the steering wheel disappearing under his massive hands.

Noticing Dimitri's astonished expression, Wolfgang broke out laughing.

"Welcome", he proclaimed in German-accented Russian. "In the car, and only in the car, we are allowed to speak Russian. Despite his size, the driver – we call him Colossus – is transparent. As far as you're concerned, he is deaf, dumb and blind. By the way, he may have the body of a bear, but he has the soul of a bird."

Dimitri could not contain his astonishment. He means a bird of prey, Dimitri thought to himself.

"He is one of our best and most experienced men. He will now drive us to a house in the city, where you will meet two more of my people, and we'll review everything tonight. The order I received is that we complete everything from start to finish before daybreak tomorrow. You have a flight to catch early tomorrow morning."

"Fine", agreed Dimitri.

The black Mercedes Benz 300 SD glided gracefully on the flawless road to the picturesque town of Siegen, and in less than an hour was already parked in front of an elegant two-story home. A high wooden fence surrounded the house on all sides. Dimitri followed Wolfgang through a black wrought-iron gate to a red brick path leading to the front door. It was already dusk and most of the windows were lit.

Wolfgang rapped on the door once. They were soon inside.

"Olga and Thomas, this is Dimitri", Wolfgang said.

Dimitri shook their hands and followed Thomas to the living room, where he seated himself in one of the oversized leather armchairs casually placed around the large room.

"Tea or coffee?" asked Olga. She was about six feet tall and wore tight gray leather trousers which emphasized her slender figure. Her smooth blond hair touched her shoulders, and her large, lustrous blue eyes shone in bright contrast to her light skin. She was a stunning Russian beauty. Or was she German?

Dimitri's gaze was fixed on her breasts, tightly packed into a short leather jacket, unbuttoned at the top to hint at what lay underneath.

Olga, seeing where Dimitri was looking, smiled at him

without admonishment.

"Sorry. Please, I apologize", he mumbled, like a boy caught red- handed. "I prefer tea, please."

Dimitri and his three hosts now sat at the dining table for a quick dinner of takeaway Chinese food. Wolfgang placed a photograph on the table of a burly young man in a street setting.

"This is the man who will answer your questions", he explained to Dimitri. "Here, tonight."

Dimitri studied the man's face. He looked about 35 years old.

"What can you tell me about him?" he asked.

Wolfgang smiled broadly while pouring himself a shot of vodka from what seemed like a fancy bottle.

"The one who can tell you more about him is Olga", he teased, grinning. "She knows him inside out."

They all burst into laughter. Olga seemed less amused.

Then Wolfgang became serious and described the man in the photo.

"The fellow is a sergeant major in the United States Army. His name is William Lance, otherwise known as Bill. He is 35 years old. He serves as a chief fire control duty operator on a Pershing surface-to-surface missile battery. His battery has been deployed in this area for just over a year. He is married with a three-year-old son, and he and his family live in a gated compound which the US army rented in the area. Olga came to know him three months ago and has already acquired a great deal of information from him about the missile battery and its operations.

"Tonight, we're playing it differently", Wolfgang continued. "Olga, who already has a date with him tonight in a bar downtown, will bring him here. We will conduct a swift, thorough questioning, after which he will be disposed of. You can also understand that this is Olga's last mission here, and that she will return to Moscow with you tomorrow morning", he informed Dimitri.

Exhaling a large breath of air, Dimitri quickly reviewed everything Wolfgang had related.

"Well done. Excellent work you've done so far", Dimitri praised Wolfgang. "A fire control operator is exactly what we need. I'm sure you know how to make him talk. I just need to ask him a few questions, and I don't need to know what you are going to do with him afterward. In fact, I actually prefer not to know."

Dimitri turned to Olga. She was perfectly calm.

"I'm sorry that because of my mission you are forced to cut short your stay here. I am sure, however, that your operators in Moscow will know how to utilize your excellent capabilities", he apologized, rather formally.

Olga thanked him with a dip of her head, and just a hint of a smile.

THE SMALL LOCAL BAR IN SIEGEN'S TINY CITY CENTER was crowded, noisy, and full of smoke. Olga sat on a stool at the bar and engaged in small talk with the bartender, whom she had known since coming to Siegen a year earlier. Wolfgang's driver sat at a table in a dark corner, drinking beer from a tall stein and watching the revelers.

A tall, dark-haired, athletically built man in his mid-thirties, wearing a western cowboy hat, approached Olga, who remained in her seat and embraced him warmly. He removed his hat and settled into a bar stool next to her. They seemed like a married couple or long-time lovers, drinking beer from tall porcelain steins, laughing and touching each other frequently. Their intimacy seemed odd to some of the customers in the bar. Americans were well liked in Siegen as good, generous customers, but the sight of a mixed couple, an American and what appeared to be a blond local beauty, caused discomfort to some, and even more to others. But Colossus was in the corner to ensure that discomfort did not escalate to violence.

BACK AT THE HOUSE, THE TELEPHONE RANG. Wolfgang picked it up. "OK, OK", he said and hung up.

"Dimitri", Wolfgang called. "It's show time.

"The fish and the bait will leave the bar in ten minutes and will come straight here. Now we need to make sure that you haven't wasted your time coming here. Right?"

Wolfgang handed Dimitri a black woolen ski mask. He gave another to Thomas and kept one for himself.

"We will all cover our faces", he directed.

"But you said that we would eliminate him anyway", Thomas protested. Wolfgang looked at Thomas as if he were a toddler.

"When will you learn, Thomas? If he sees our faces, he will understand right away that he is not coming out alive and he will not talk. With our faces covered, he will sing right away, as he will assume that we will release him after he gives us answers."

Wolfgang was an old hand in the business of getting people to talk.

"Now", he said to Thomas, "Turn off all the lights and open the window in the living room. We need to hear them when they come. Hurry!"

Dimitri looked at Thomas. This is a man who does not

attract attention and does not leave an impression, Dimitri thought. He was of medium height with bland facial features; balding, bespectacled. A postal clerk type.

The hum of a car engine sounded through the open window as the car came to a stop. They heard doors opening and closing and a cheerful, giggly exchange between a man and a woman heading for the house. Soon the door opened, and the man drawled in a loud deep voice, "After you, ma'am."

"Thank you for being such a gentleman, but it's dark and you'd better go in first", demurred the woman, who was Olga.

The man entered cautiously in total darkness, groping the wall in search of a light switch. Then suddenly a bright flash, similar to lighting, lit the room for a moment, followed by a scorching sound and chirping. The man dropped to the floor like a sack of potatoes.

"Hurry, hurry", sounded a voice. It was Wolfgang. "Thomas, quick, turn the light on. Let's drag him to the pantry."

The lights went on. The two struggled to move the unconscious Sergeant Major William "Bill" Lance.

Dimitri sought out Olga. She was sitting in an armchair in the living room, looking out and smoking a cigarette. She was calm, as if she had just returned home from a boring evening with a date. There was nothing in her demeanor that hinted that she knew that the bore she had just dated, married and a father, on a military career path, would be dead within an hour, at most.

Colossus appeared at the door, closing and locking it. He walked briskly to his business in the pantry. He will not miss an opportunity, Dimitri thought, to refresh his skills of subduing an enemy, squeezing information out of him for dear life, killing him humanely and disposing of him without leaving a trace. It was an activity that would give him a great sense of accomplishment.

Dimitri followed Colossus to the pantry, which contained a few cans of food on the shelves, a rusty old bicycle and a collection of unwanted household items. Bill Lance, all six feet four inches of him, was seated on a massive wooden chair. His arms and feet were bound with canvas straps to the chair's armrests and legs. He was heaving, not yet awake.

Dimitri was concerned. "Wolfgang", he implored, constantly searching for a sign of life in the prisoner's face, "I hope your electric shocker did not finish him off completely. He seems halfway to paradise to me."

"Trust me", Wolfgang replied resolutely, while tightening the straps on the man's feet. "From experience, within four minutes he will be up and singing."

Bill Lance began to regain consciousness, coughing and moving his head from side to side. Thomas appeared from nowhere with a small bucket and poured its contents of ice water over the prisoner's head. The Sergeant Major gasped, opened his eyes and looked up. He appeared to be trying to get up from his chair, but the chair was solidly bolted to the floor. He was struggling. He looked up fearfully at the four hooded men who surrounded him.

"What the hell!" exclaimed the American.

None of the captors responded.

"I swear", implored the American soldier, "by my wife and son, that I will never again date a German woman. I swear.

"Now let me go", he pleaded. "Please."

"Sergeant Major Bill Lance, shut your mouth", Wolfgang barked in heavily accented English. "You wish we were Fascist. If we were neo- Nazis, you would be much better off. Your adultery is against the rules of your military but of no interest to us. We are here tonight to discuss with you a rather technical subject, Pershing missiles. Have you heard about them? If we have time left, we can discuss your infidelities later."

Sergeant Major Lance fell silent, taking in the turn of events and the severity of his grim situation. He then returned to his senses and tried his utmost to be as professional as he thought was expected of him.

"My Name is William Keith Lance, Sergeant Major in the United States Army, serial number 353-40-1733."

Wolfgang reached into his coat's inner pocket and pulled out a handgun. It was a SIG Sauer P220 with a built-in silencer. He cocked it and slowly directed it at the American, bringing it closer to his face.

"So it is you, Rambo", Wolfgang snarled in a mocking voice. "OK, Rambo, listen up. You have only two options. One option is that we leave the room, put in earplugs, and let you negotiate your fate with this gorilla", he said, pointing at Colossus.

The non-commissioned officer gazed at Colossus, who stood facing him with folded arms.

"The second option is that we skip the first part and get straight to work", offered Wolfgang.

Dimitri watched the scene as if he were in a theater, not believing his eyes. Wolfgang aimed the barrel of his pistol at the American's left knee and pulled the trigger. A faint puff and the gun action sounded, and through the pungent smoke, Dimitri could see that the nine- millimeter round had pierced the knee of his subject, who screamed in agony. His face was contorted with pain and his eyes looked as though they would pop out of their sockets. His chest was heaving uncontrollably. As if this was not enough, Wolfgang hit the American's head with the pistol.

Wolfgang seemed to be in his element when torturing his captive. Dimitri feared that Wolfgang was risking the prisoner's life before he could be interrogated, but kept his thoughts to himself.

"You are making too much noise", snarled Wolfgang, "and it really is annoying to everybody, especially to your girlfriend in the other room. I thought we could have a laugh together, but now I give you only two options to choose from, right now. The first is that you start talking now, and do it quickly, before you bleed out, because, unfortunately, I don't have any bandages left. The second option is that I tell you that we are short of time, and my way of hinting is to put a bullet in your other knee."

Wolfgang was now aiming the pistol at the American's right knee. His captive's eyes were clenched shut in agony and he was weeping profusely. It would break the heart of any man, but not of his tormentor.

"Don't do it, please. Please", begged the captive. "I'll tell you all you want to know."

Dimitri, who was afraid that Wolfgang's finest moments would cost him valuable information, approached Wolfgang and whispered in his ear.

"He is mine now", Dimitri said.

Dimitri grabbed a chair and dragged it towards the American. He sat very close to his subject, a few inches from his face. Wolfgang spoke again.

"Sergeant Major, my friend will now ask you several questions that you will answer truthfully. Any wrong answer will cost you another bullet in the leg, and then we will move up your body. Just take into account that I have only two magazines of ammunition. Is that clear?"

"Yes, sir" mumbled the sergeant major unintelligibly. "What is your job in the battery?"

"I am a non-commissioned officer in the battery fire control unit, Sir."

"Do you, or does anyone else in the battery, have the capacity to independently launch a missile?"

"I can launch, sir, but the missile will have no target." "What do you mean by 'no target'?"

Struggling to answer, the sergeant major did his best to keep his voice steady.

"In order for the missile to hit a specific target, we need to input a code that we receive with the order from the United States Army Headquarters here in West Germany, Sir."

"You mean to say, Sergeant, that you have no preselected targets and codes in the battery's safe box in case of an emergency?"

The American again struggled to produce a reply. Wolfgang barked again.

"Do you want me to help you think with the other knee?"

"No, Sir. No, we have nothing like that in peacetime", the captive answered. "This is the truth, I swear to you, Sir", he implored.

Dimitri continued his interrogation. He was now growing convinced that his trip had been for nothing, and that he would return empty- handed to Moscow and to a dressing-down by Marshal Budarenko.

"I am asking you again, Sergeant Major Lance. Do you or do you not have target codes on site for use in case of severed communications? What happens if headquarters are bombed or invaded?"

"Then it is totally impossible to launch, Sir", the captive

answered faintly. "Emergency regulations require delivery of target codes to the battery only when DEFCON 2 alert is announced, but even then..." He stopped speaking and closed his eyes.

"Go on, Sergeant, go on!" Wolfgang ordered.

"Why did you stop? You want to talk from the hole in your mouth or the hole in your knee?" Wolfgang was obviously delighted.

The Sergeant Major was struggling to contain his pain. A small pool of blood was forming at his feet. He was shivering.

"Even though we input the target data to the missile, Sir, we still need the High Command's OK to actually launch", he managed to sputter out.

"Sergeant Major", insisted Dimitri, "you said you can launch a missile without entering the code. What happens to the missile then?"

"If the missile is launched without a code and a selected target, it self-destructs when reaching its highest point outside the atmosphere."

Dimitri saw no need to question the American any further.

Sergeant Major Lance, who had probably gone through interrogation training, had slowly come to realize that he was of no more value to his captors. He started describing his wife and three-year-old son, begging for mercy. Dimitri left the room quietly and the rest of the men followed him.

The captive was left alone in the room, weeping in agony.

Wolfgang called Colossus, his driver and special mission operative.

"This Yank did not really help. Our important guest will be leaving empty-handed. Waste the Yank, get rid of his car and clean the room. You know what to do."

"I've made tea for you", Olga said to Dimitri as he entered the living room. Dimitri noticed that she had changed her clothes and combed her hair. She looked like a different woman. What is she made of, this woman, Dimitri wondered? Probably forged steel. Her consort of the night was being wasted at this very moment, and she could not be calmer or less seductive.

Wolfgang entered, glancing at his watch.

"Comrades", he announced in his German-accented Russian. "It's already a quarter to four in the morning. We must move out of here quickly and head straight to the airport. There's going to be a lot of commotion here very soon. I believe the Yank's wife has already reported his disappearance to the military police. When they understand that he is a senior operator of a nuclear missile battery, the *Bundesamt für Verfassungsschutz*[5] will start digging and turning over every stone, including every outgoing flight. They will all be looking for one thing in particular – Olga's pretty skull. We must go now. Thomas, help with the cleaning here. I'll drive them to the airport."

THE THREE ENTERED THE TERMINAL GATE OF THE SLEEPY airport. Only a few passengers were present, most of them slumped on their benches awaiting their flights. Wolfgang tapped Dimitri's shoulder.

"I really don't like it that you're arriving and leaving from the same airport", Wolfgang commented. "It's against the rules, but we have no choice. You have to get out of here as quickly as you can. Now give me your passport", he said, while handing Dimitri a new one. "This is your new passport. It's

---

5   German Federal Internal Secret Service

OK. It has an entry stamp from last week and also an exit stamp from Moscow. Just remember your new name, and that you came to Germany a week ago. That's all."

Dimitri examined his new British passport and practiced his new name, Robert Hugh Pearson. He suddenly felt alarmed.

"According to their registration, the old passport will not have an exit stamp. It will cause problems, won't it?" he asked Wolfgang.

Wolfgang smiled at him, patting him on the shoulder.

"You can start working with us. You are right, but this will be taken care of. Now stay here, you and Olga, while I book you on the earliest departing flight. I also want to remind you not to sit next to each other during the flight."

He collected the passports from Dimitri and Olga and walked away quickly. Dimitri tried to start a conversation with Olga, but she was not in a talkative mood.

Wolfgang returned, waving flight tickets. "It's Austrian Airlines flight 192. Departure in thirty-five minutes", he told them, looking at his watch.

"You should arrive in Vienna by seven o'clock. Here are the tickets, including those for your connecting flight to Moscow. You must board right away – boarding closes in ten minutes", Wolfgang instructed them, handing them the tickets.

Dimitri shook Wolfgang's hand firmly and thanked him. Wolfgang kissed Olga on the cheek, turned away and walked briskly out the terminal gate.

THE AUSTRIAN AIRLINES DC-9 TOUCHED DOWN ON THE SNOWY tarmac of Vienna International Airport. Dimitri hurried to the Aeroflot counter in the departures terminal, keeping sight of Olga, who walked a little ahead of him. There was a large crowd there, which alerted Dimitri's instincts to something irregular. He made his way through several people in front of him, and handed his ticket to the Aeroflot ticketing agent at the counter, but she returned it to him almost immediately.

"I am sorry, sir, but no flights are departing due to a heavy snowstorm in Moscow. All three international airports in Moscow have already been closed for two hours, and it may be a long time before they reopen", she explained, handing him a voucher. "This is for the NH Wien Hotel right here in the airport, and you can either walk there or take a shuttle to the door. Check in there and we will notify you of the next available flight."

Dimitri took the voucher and the ticket and put them in the pocket of his bag. He thanked the agent and walked out the exit door. He could see Olga just ahead of him, carrying a small suitcase. He quickened his pace until he reached her.

"Excuse me, miss", he said. Olga turned to him.

"If I'm not mistaken, I've seen you before, at the Aeroflot counter. Did they send you to the NH Wien too?"

Olga nodded.

"It's almost a kilometer away. Can I help you with the suitcase?" "Absolutely", Olga replied, and passed the suitcase to him, keeping her expression as frozen as the frigid weather surrounding them.

THEY REACHED THE BROWNSTONE FACADE OF THE HOTEL, and within minutes Olga had already checked in and was walking to the elevators. Several minutes later, Dimitri did the same.

He was surprised to see Olga was still waiting for an elevator. It doesn't make sense, he thought, that the elevator was taking so long. Could it be that Olga was waiting for him?

It seemed as if the few minutes in the well-heated hotel lobby had thawed out the ice from Olga's face, as she gave a beaming smile when she saw Dimitri.

"So, what do we do now? It could take an hour, or a day or two", she asked Dimitri.

Dimitri looked at her with surprise. It was the first time he had seen her acting naturally, without the mask she had worn since he had first met her. It was also the first time that he heard her speak in Russian. A "new Olga" was unfolding before him.

"Let's pass the time together, drink something, shower, and wait for a call from the airport. I don't trust the Aeroflot people. I think we need to call them every two hours, just in case", he suggested.

"You're right", agreed Olga. "If it takes longer, maybe we should sleep in shifts. You know, like in the army."

Dimitri smiled.

"Soldiers would love to serve in these conditions", he suggested. Olga let out a sweet smile. She leaned over to his ear and whispered.

"All right, we'll spend the time together, in my room, but on one condition. You don't ask me anything about my work, or anything personal, and vice versa. Agreed?"

"Agreed", replied Dimitri and pressed the elevator button to Olga's floor.

Once in the room, Olga headed straight to the bathroom. She opened all the soap and cream bottles and tested them. "Would you like some tea?" she heard Dimitri ask her from the bedroom.

"I'll have a hot bath first. Then I'd love some tea."

Olga shut the bathroom door and turned on the tap, filling the tub with steaming hot water. Dimitri changed into a pair of gym shorts and sank into an armchair. Within seconds, he was dozing off. He had had almost no rest in the past 24 hours, four cities and four airports ago.

He awakened suddenly and reached for his watch to see how long he had been asleep, when he noticed Olga standing by a mirror in the corner. She stood naked, facing the large mirror, wearing only a tiny pair of underpants. To avoid embarrassment, he closed his eyes and pretended to be asleep.

"We haven't even planned the shifts and you're already asleep", Olga called out from the mirror. "You can open your eyes now. It's OK. I think something was said about a cup of tea."

Dimitri opened his eyes. Olga was standing exactly where she had been a few minutes earlier. She was rubbing her face with cream, seemingly devoted to this task. Dimitri could not take his eyes off of her. He then noticed a long scar on her back, right under her right shoulder.

"You haven't answered me", she said. "Is your tongue still working??"

Dimitri was trying to answer when Olga turned away from the mirror and faced him, revealing the length of her naked body and the splendor of her breasts. Dimitri turned his eyes away, but she walked to the king- sized bed, pulled the bed cover to the floor, and snuggled between the sheets, all the while looking at Dimitri, who had no idea how to respond.

"Are you going to stay there, Brigadier General?" she challenged him.

He was surprised to hear her reciting his military rank, as he had not revealed it to her or her companions back in

Siegen. He recalled the woman who had followed him out of Moscow, through Zurich and on to Cologne. Is that what this is? That woman completed her mission in Cologne, and now my new follower is Olga. He had no doubt.

Olga saw that he was thinking, and spoke again.

"I will not be insulted if you tell me that you don't like me", she assured him.

Dimitri quickly returned to his senses. Military rank, surveillance, whatever it may be, was a small price to pay for this opportunity. Or maybe not. Olga was almost impossible to resist. He smiled broadly at her.

"I do like you. I think you are – how to say it – perfect!" he proclaimed.

"I must say that I enjoyed watching you while you were napping. You seem to like sports."

She pulled out the edge of the sheet, and motioned for him to join her. Dimitri came nearer, but Olga suddenly broke into laughter.

"We are not in gymnastics class. Can you remove those ridiculous shorts before joining me in bed?"

He pulled down his shorts and entered the bed. He pulled her to him and embraced her tightly.

"I see you want to smother me, but maybe we should make love first", she suggested.

Dimitri was not totally at ease. He smiled briefly and loosened his embrace. He kissed her on the lips and she held him longer and closer. He caressed her long body, and touched the scar under her shoulder. Olga stopped her giggling.

"It looks like an operational accident, and whoever treated you was not a doctor. Maybe a car mechanic", Dimitri observed.

Olga smiled.

"This question belongs in the realm of subjects that we do not discuss. Remember?"

"Yes, indeed", Dimitri assented, and kissed her on the lips.

Then he got up, pulled the curtains shut, and returned to the bed. They both needed to unwind, which they did.

THE TELEPHONE RANG LOUDLY. DIMITRI JUMPED OUT OF BED and held the receiver to his ear. "Thank you", he said and hung up.

Olga watched him. "Any news?"

"Yes", said Dimitri. "Our neighbors have complained to the reception desk that we are too noisy."

"Really, Brigadier General? Was it from Aeroflot?"

"Yes. The truth is that I want to stay here forever with you, but Moscow is calling. They said that Domodedovo airport will probably open soon. We have to be at the airport within two hours. Let's get up now, and shower, my dear."

OLGA STOOD JUST BEHIND DIMITRI IN THE LONG LINE FOR the Aeroflot desk at Vienna Airport. Dimitri felt that she was playing games with him, taking advantage of the crowded conditions to rub against him frequently.

She came close to him, bit his earlobe lightly and whispered in his ear.

"You remember the rules. I will sit two to three rows behind you in the cabin."

IT WAS SNOWING IN MOSCOW. DIMITRI WALKED TO THE CURB outside the grand arrival terminal of Domodedovo airport. He immediately noticed a young man who had been part of the team of soldiers guarding the secret think tank at the base outside Moscow. Dimitri motioned to the soldier, who came to him and took his overnight bag. He then turned to Olga to say goodbye, but she had changed again; she was now icy. He reached out to her for a handshake.

"Thank you for your service. I hope we meet again someday", he said. She did not shake his hand.

"Don't count on it", she snapped, spinning on her heels and striding away.

CHAPTER 4

THE BLACK LADA CAR DROVE THROUGH THE GATES OF THE SECRET ARMY BASE. In the car, Brigadier General Dimitri was deep in thoughts that gave him no respite. He felt sorry for the disappointment that would soon be felt by his fellow teammates, who had had such high hopes for his trip to Germany. I can only hope that one of them has somehow been able to come up with a creative idea, he said to himself – an idea that will spare us from the claws of that hungry and impatient bear, Marshal Budarenko.

When he arrived at the conference room, it looked almost the same as when he had left it. His five colleagues were leaning over their desks, but this time, documents and maps were scattered all over in disarray. The moment he entered, his colleagues stopped whatever they were doing and greeted him.

It was the slender Colonel Yevgeni, the physicist, who wasted no time. He turned to Dimitri in his typical, direct way.

"So Brigadier General", the Colonel asked. "Have we made progress, or only progressed on our sure path to the guillotine?"

Dimitri looked at him sharply. From the way he presented his question, the Brigadier General reasoned, it was safe to assume that the team had not made any progress. Therefore,

Yevgeni's macabre humor was totally inadequate, not to say unproductive, in their present situation.

"I'm glad that you are keeping up our morale, Colonel", said Dimitri. "The good guys there actually fulfilled all their promises; they are a capable team. Unfortunately, in my interview with a sergeant major from the Pershing missile battery, it turned out that they have no independent launch capacity, just as it is with the submarines. I'm sorry to disappoint you, Colonel, but that's how it is."

The Brigadier paused and then asked, "And what about you here? Have you come up with any idea, or a new direction?"

Yevgeni preferred to ignore Dimitri's deflecting question. He continued his debriefing.

"Just a minute, Brigadier General. Let me understand. Did you interview that NCO from the Pershing battery yourself?" he asked.

"Yes. I did", replied Dimitri.

"And how can you be sure that he didn't pull a trick on you?"

"Colonel Yevgeni, he was in no position to make jokes. If you were him, and first thing, even before you were asked the first question, you had your knee smashed with a nine millimeter bullet, would you not begin to reveal everything you know in detail? I only had to ask the questions and our good fellows in Germany made sure that his answers were true and sincere."

Yevgeni nodded. He had no appetite for gore.

"I understand", he said. "Regarding your question, we checked several new directions, which we later had to rule out. Oh, and by the way, the Minister is about to arrive here. It seems that because of your absence, he did not come to meet us yesterday. On the other hand, after two days, I assume that his level of expectation from us, and the inevitable disappointment, will be greater than usual. I am sorry, but at the moment, I don't think we have anything to sell to him."

"Sell to him?" Dimitri snapped impatiently. "He takes everything for free, and that includes our heads as well."

Colonel Yevgeni was now lost in his own thoughts. His head rested on his hands, which were on the table, and he was obviously concentrating.

He sat like this for a long time, when suddenly he straightened up and turned to Dimitri, who was across the table from him.

"Listen", he said. "I have a feeling that I will be able to get at least a temporary reprieve from the Minister of Defense, maybe a few days."

Hearing this, Dimitri rushed to Colonel Yevgeni, sat next to him and, in a gesture of friendship, wrapped his arm around the colonel's bony shoulder.

"Go on, I'm listening", he said.

Colonel Yevgeni did not seem ready yet, as he was trying to put his thoughts in order and to weigh his words very carefully before spelling out the idea that he was formulating.

"Do you remember that the first idea that we came up with, which was ruled out, was the American nuclear submarines?"

"Do I remember? Of course I remember. It was my idea and it was I who brought it up."

"I'm not really sure, because it is still a very raw idea", said Yevgeni. "But I decided to revisit the submarine scenario. My intention is to isolate…"

He was interrupted as the door was flung wide open and there stood Gregory, described not long before by Minister of Defense as the "father and mother of the think tank". He motioned quickly to the six

Red Army officers in the room to rise to their feet and stand at attention. In what had by now become a familiar ritual, within seconds, the Minister of Defense, hero of the Soviet Union, Marshal Budarenko, marched swiftly inside. This time the marshal seated himself at the table on the raised platform, and instructed the team to take their seats. He gazed at Dimitri.

"Brigadier General Dimitri, when did you return and with what?"

Dimitri stood up at attention.

"Mr. Minister, I returned an hour ago."

"Did you accomplish your mission?" asked the minister.

"It was efficient, but not entirely effective", replied the brigadier. The Minister of Defense raised his bushy eyebrows, perplexed. "Your choice of definition is very… interesting. Explain!"

The brigadier took a deep breath.

"Sir, it was efficient in everything to do with the execution of the mission. The right subject was located, captured, interviewed, and all was done within a few hours. However, the outcome was not good, as during the interrogation it became apparent to me that in the Pershing battery, firing the missile is enabled quite simply and easily, but the missile would have no target. Here, just like in the submarines, the battery must receive a certain code from the high command of the American forces in Germany in advance. Only when the state of alert is raised to one degree below total war, only then do the batteries receive the codes, which are stored in the battery's safe box. Even then, it would become a problem to execute a firing, as in a state of such high alert, it would be all but impossible to penetrate with a clandestine operation, occupy the battery and execute a missile launch. Unfortunately, the bottom line is that it is impractical."

Dimitri finished speaking and waited for the minister's permission to return to his seat, but permission was not granted and he remained standing while the Minister, ominously, did not speak. The silence in the room contrasted with his normal thundering, boisterous, commanding manner. All that time, the Minister was tapping on the table with his right hand. He was restless.

"Sit down now, Brigadier", the minister finally snapped. "According to the last report I received from Gregory, up to this minute, your total collective outcome is zero. Z-E-R-O."

The minister roared the last word, hitting the table with great force with his fist. Marshal Budarenko had a mercurial temper at the best of times – his propensity to anger was notorious throughout the Soviet Union, and the fear of his wrath made his subordinates, and even his few superiors, do their best to please or placate him. For the think tank members, at least for five of the six, who were sitting opposite him, it was their first experience of it firsthand. Marshal Budarenko's wrath made them fear for their lives.

Then the minister pulled a white handkerchief out of his pocket, buried his flat nose in it, and emitted a thunderous blow. The team members, who were all senior Red Army and Navy officers, felt like schoolchildren, following every motion with anxiety, as if trying to decipher in the notes that he was producing, while blowing his nose, something of the fate awaiting them. Then the Marshal put the handkerchief back in his pocket and gazed at the team again.

"Six zeros. You are simply six zeros", the minister concluded his evaluation.

He turned his gaze to Gregory, who sat closest to him.

"Maybe it's not their fault. You know what teachers write in the evaluation sheet of an intellectually limited pupil at the end of the school year? They write, 'He did the best he could'. Maybe this is all that these people can actually do. They are not at fault for being dim, but the one who selected them is, and that is you – Gregory!"

Gregory stood up when the Marshal addressed him and he remained standing, motionless, knowing the Minister would eventually come to his senses. I must keep quiet and absorb the Minister's abuse with submission, he said to himself. Every word I try to say will only worsen my situation.

"If this is the situation, then I will change my plans", thundered the Minister. "Instead of replacing any one of you with another member from the reserve team, I will put the entire reserve team into action, all six of them, and you, all of you, I will just…"

The minister raised his right hand opposite the faces of the team members, rubbing his rough, stubby fingers as if grinding a clod of dirt into powder and blowing it to the wind.

"… and you I will scatter away."

To Colonel Yevgeni and to his teammates, the Minister's dramatic display of crushing a grain of dirt and blowing it to the wind seemed more like the scattering of their ashes after their untimely death. But then Yevgeni stood up from his seat opposite the Minister, who seemed momentarily shocked, just like every team member in the room. The Minister looked at the thin, bespectacled Colonel, who had not been granted permission to do whatever he was intending to do.

"Colonel Yevgeni, what's come over you? Do you want to perform a trick on me now, trying to save your head?"

"No, Mr. Minister", said Yevgeni in a hushed tone. "I have an idea which has been keeping me preoccupied since yesterday. I didn't want to tell this to anybody, not even to Gregory, before I could check if this idea can be done, if it is feasible and executable, and what its probability of success is, not just in execution, but also in producing the desired outcome. In fact, I will present two different plans. One is easy and quick to execute but has one critical point that requires investigation. The second plan is complex and may be cumbersome and will require preliminary testing; however…"

The Minister interrupted Yevgeni angrily.

"Then don't present me with the complex and cumbersome plan. You disqualify it just by saying it's complex,."

Dimitri watched Yevgeni. He could only be impressed by the conduct and bearing of a man whose appearance completely belied his character. Yevgeni was not just very clever; he had courage.

"Mr. Minister, the second plan is indeed complex and will require time for testing, but in my opinion, this plan can be the ultimate operation. It will take me about twenty minutes to explain both plans without going into detail. If the Honorable Minister is in a hurry, I can present the data to Gregory first and he will…"

The Minister looked at his watch in disdain and looked at Yevgeni again.

"Now Colonel, don't try to run my schedule. You have fifteen minutes precisely. Carry on."

Yevgeni breathed a little easier and immediately proceeded to present his plans.

"In the first plan, we would send a bomber from our Air Force to fly at low altitude, under our radar cover and that of the Americans. The bomber will enter Alaska, turn back and pull up to a high altitude and execute the precise attack flight path that we know, the same one that the American B-52 bombers have been practicing for years. Then, we fly out of Alaska in our direction, as if to Siberia, and practice firing nuclear missiles at the east of our country. This work can be done with one Tupolev 22 bomber, which will fire a nuclear missile into a relatively barren area in eastern Siberia. We can create effects or elements around this that will lend reliability to this action, to look as if it were an American attack, a belligerent act using nuclear weapons on our territory. We can, for example, alert our anti-aircraft missile batteries of an American bomber that is about to enter our airspace that is equipped with all our radar and friend or foe codes. This way we ensure that our anti-aircraft missile batteries shoot down the Tupolev 22 when it returns from Alaska and is detected entering our airspace.

"We can continue to reinforce our cover story to seem totally reliable."

"Go on, Colonel", Marshal Budarenko was beginning to show curiosity, though still glancing at his watch.

"We can, for example, send our friends in Vietnam a transport plane that will bring real fragments of an American B-52 bomber from there. They have plenty of those. We then plant them in the field and on treetops, and the media would have a feast.

"This plan is very easy to execute; however, it has one big flaw. Half the world, including everybody in the Soviet Union and in the Kremlin, would actually believe that it was an American attack; on the other hand, the other half of the world, especially the Americans, will know for certain that it is a conspiracy. If we add to that the vast armored forces that we will concentrate in the west of the country, I have no doubt that the Americans will understand that this is a deception and they will call a red alert. This way they will face us ahead of time, ready for action, even before we start our ground operations in Western Europe."

Colonel Yevgeni paused, took a sip of water, and looked intently at the Minister of Defense, trying to decipher the level of interest or any sign of curiosity for the plan that he had just laid out.

"Okay, I understand", the minister said matter-of-factly and scratched his head. "And what is the second plan, that you think can be perfect? "

Yevgeni quickly drank some more water before he continued.

"In the second plan, I am actually going back to the American nuclear submarines. The goal is to employ sophisticated means of deception to cause an American submarine to launch a real nuclear missile into our territory. If this really happens, and the Americans will be certain that it is indeed their submarine which attacked us, then our ground invasion of Western Europe will be totally justified. We need to find one such submarine that is navigating underwater in the North Sea, not very far from Soviet territory, and they do conduct quite a few of these navigation exercises. The purpose is to create an effect near the submarine that simulates a nuclear blast. The precise location of the blast must be such that it will provide the submarine with data of a big nuclear explosion that has taken place far from them. The course to the epicenter of the blast will lead to the United States of America. This means that for the submarine, all data would indicate a nuclear attack on American soil."

Yevgeni then reached for the glass of water and drank the rest of it in one big gulp. He cleared his throat and spoke again.

"Now I am getting to the two main points. From my experience in the field, I know that a nuclear explosion causes an immediate communication block that lasts for quite a long time. We will create this communication block, or simulate it by means of electronic warfare. Maybe even combine this with aerial scattering of metal chaff, similar to that which is used for jamming radars. The captain of the submarine that we target will also know that a nuclear explosion causes a communication block. The result will be that he would be unable to contact his headquarters in the US, another indication that his homeland has indeed been attacked by nuclear weapons. All that this submarine captain can do is what he was trained to do in his many years of training, and that is to launch a Trident missile or a batch of missiles at us. This is more or less the plan, Mr. Minister."

Marshal Budarenko lit a cigarette and leaned back in his chair.

"Colonel Yevgeni, come here and stand by me."

Yevgeni seemed deeply ill at ease, but he hurried to stand beside the minister. His posture was the antithesis of a military man and he tried, without success, to stop his hands from shaking. The minister noticed it.

"It looks to me, Colonel, that you must be threatened into creativity", said the minister to Yevgeni, who heaved a sigh of relief.

"Mr. Minister", said the colonel meekly, "can I also light a cigarette?"

All the officers in the room froze. Yevgeni's request was contrary to Russian military culture, violating every convention, and it meant only one thing: untold insubordination. Gregory, the think tank supervisor and ethics authority, looked livid. The other officers looked on in disbelief as the Minister passed his own pack of Marlboro Reds to Yevgeni.

'Thank you, Sir, but I have my own cigarettes", Yevgeni mumbled. "I only wanted to know if I, too, can smoke here in the room."

"Take one, take, Colonel!" the Minister commanded. "It seems that at least today, you've earned one good American cigarette. For tomorrow, we shall wait and see."

Yevgeni immediately felt the metaphorical lead weights lifting from his shulders. His hand shook when he held the Marlboro box and pulled out a single cigarette, which he kept unlit between his fingers. The Minister watched his every move, passing his fingers through his hair in a familiar gesture.

"The first plan can be executed quickly, even within hours", said the Minister, "and this is probably its biggest advantage. On the other hand, you also noted its limits. For now, it seems that we will proceed with the second plan, but before we do this, I want you to list all, but all, its weaknesses. I'm waiting."

Yevgeni recomposed himself quickly. He was no longer shaking and his voice was steady.

"Mr. Minister, I truly do not believe that there is any problem in execution. I am certain it will work, but the problem is with the schedule. We would require assistance in the matter from our Electronic Warfare corps. We would have to conduct several explosions at sea and document the effects. We also have to practice it on one of our nuclear submarines, so it is difficult for me to tell you just how many days it will take, but I give you my word, the word of an officer in the Red Army, that we shall do it in the best and quickest way possible."

The Minister of Defense was enjoying every drag of his

cigarette as he listened intently to every word.

"So you give me the word of an officer", he said, "and that is good. And I tell you that from this moment, you, Colonel, are selected to lead this plan, even though your team includes officers who are more senior than you. Is that clear to you, General Vitaly Okhramenko?"

The General leapt onto his feet from among the team members sitting before the Minister.

"Yes, Mr. Minister!"

The officers in the team had not yet gotten to know one another very well, and they had not been properly introduced, mostly because, so far, the main work had been done by Colonel Yevgeni and Brigadier General Dimitri; so it came as a great surprise to them that the short, fat older fellow was a Red Army General.

"I have a surprise for you, Colonel Yevgeni", the Minister said, leaning back.

"We have invested a lot of brainpower in selecting the team members and their specialties. If you have not discovered yet, General Okhramenko is one of the leading experts in electronic warfare in the Red Army, and probably in the world. If you guide him correctly with data, he will solve all your problems in this area."

Yevgeni, still standing beside the general, mumbled some words of gratitude.

"Wait, I'm not finished yet", the marshal said. "Colonel Nazarbayev!"

Again, the five team members shifted their gaze to Colonel Nazarbayev, who snapped to attention and called out: "Yes, Mr. Minister".

Colonel Nazarbayev had the build of a wrestler. His round

head and narrow eyes, as well as his name, revealed his Kazakh origins.

"Colonel Yevgeni", the minister roared. "What is going on with you? Are you a pack of lone wolves? Do you think only you and Dimitri have a role here and all the others are just observers? It is time you got to learn about one another. Colonel Nazarbayev is a well-known expert in ordnance, warheads, and explosives. I think you have someone here that you can run with. This time tomorrow, we shall meet here again. I will bring some experts with me and we shall analyze all the aspects of this operation together; all the advantages and disadvantages of your plan, Yevgeni."

It was the first time that the Minister called someone by his first name without preceding it with his military rank.

The Minister rose, followed by everyone else. He hurried to the door, closely followed by Gregory.

Dimitri, who only a few hours before had returned from Germany and felt tired, approached Yevgeni and tapped him on the shoulder.

"Did you see that motion that the Minister made with his fingers of how he would scatter us?"

"Did I see? Of course I did. How could I not see?"

Dimitri smiled at Yevgeni and again tapped him on the shoulder.

"As partners in the same fate, I want to thank you for saving our skins for at least a few more hours. In my opinion, you are a genius. You are a true genius. By the way, how long have you been a smoker?"

"Since yesterday", Yevgeni replied with a half-smile. "From the moment you took off for Germany and left me here alone. At least now I can say that the Minister and I smoke together."

CHAPTER 5

COLONEL YEVGENI'S FIVE COLLEAGUES SEATED THEMSELVES at their desks. Yevgeni motioned to Brigadier General Dimitri with his hand to take the seat to his right, and when he did, turned to him and whispered in his ear.

"I need you close to me. You have a primary role in our plan. You are a Navy man and only you understand what happens above and below the water. My own knowledge of water begins and ends at the level of a daily shower."

Dimitri smiled and replied in a whisper.

"I will make you a certified seaman, don't you worry. Now that we know each other a little better, maybe you can tell me what the expertise of the sixth man is? Regarding Sergei, the Minister's assistant, I assume that he is here in the capacity of the minister's eyes and ears or what may be called a nark, but the sixth man is really a mystery. He makes comments every once in a while, but my impression is that he has nothing concrete to offer and that he has no specific expertise. What is your impression of him?"

A wry smile appeared on Yevgeni's face.

"Look, we are a team of experts, right? The sixth man gives the impression of being a bit of an expert in a bit of everything. This is usually the expertise of KGB men. Or he may belong to our host's military intelligence. In my opinion, he supervises us on their behalf. We need to include him more so that he doesn't get suspicions of our real roles in the team. Okay, let's start the meeting – everybody's watching us."

"Good morning", Yevgeni said, quickly scanning his colleagues' faces.

"This is not our first meeting, but it is the first that will yield a specific detailed plan, and we have a lot of work to do. But before we start, I have two comments. Yesterday, we were all clutching our heads, but it must be clear to everyone that not much has changed since yesterday. This is a large and complex plan and I have no doubt that many moments of desperation and failures await us.

"The Minister is coming back here tomorrow, this time with more experts. In my estimation, these will be Navy men or operations research specialists."

"Or both", Dimitri added.

"You are right, Dimitri. The Navy men, you know how to deal with. As for the others, we don't know if they will question us on the very technical points, or if the Minister will include them in an open discussion in order to examine all the ramifications of such an operation. We have three issues, in three different areas. Let's start with you, Colonel Nazarbayev."

The Kazakh colonel was attentive.

"The blast that will be carried out at a certain distance from the American submarine must have one purpose only: to cause its crew to think that a nuclear explosion has occurred on the East Coast of the United States. I will be more specific. We need to execute a small blast that is far enough from the submarine for the submarine not to hear the blast itself, but near enough for it to detect signals from a seismological station that indicate a nuclear explosion or an earthquake.

"In my estimation, if we catch such an American submarine in the North Sea, then our blast should indicate to them that an explosion has occurred about six thousand nautical miles from them. This is a huge distance. You, Colonel Nazarbayev, will also tell us whether an undersea blast or an explosion above sea water should be made. You should call up the brightest mathematicians and operations research specialists to carry out the calculations that will produce two clear and explicit answers. One, what should be the magnitude of the blast? Two, precisely at what distance from the submarine should it be made? Regarding the location of the blast in relation to the submarine, obviously, it depends on where we catch it. If the submarine is on its way to the North Sea, then the explosion should take place behind here and west of here, as if it is happening on United States soil. Am I clear so far?"

Colonel Nazarbayev followed Yevgeni's explanation attentively, while taking notes in his notebook in his dense handwriting. He then placed his pencil on the table and combed through his close-cut hair with his fingers, trying to concentrate before he spoke.

"Yes, Colonel Yevgeni, you are clear, but there are quite a few problems. On one hand, a small blast will not create the seismological effect that we want the submarine to detect. On the other hand, a large explosion will do that, but then it would have to be executed much farther away from the submarine so that the blast's acoustic noise does not reach it. In short, it is a table with two curves, one going up and the other going down, and we must find the right point at which the curves intersect each other. In my opinion, and at this stage I am going only by intuition, I believe that we will need to execute a large blast, using one to one-and-a-half tons of TNT, some tens of kilometers behind the submarine."

It was now Brigadier General Dimitri's turn to speak.

"Colonel Nazarbayev, do we have any such bombs of this weight in the

Navy, or even in the Air Force?"

"Yes", replied Colonel Nazarbayev. "The Air Force has such bombs, but I'm not even sure that we need them. I think that to create the seismic effect, the blast should be made on the sea bed. Therefore, I think that we should perhaps use several depth charges clustered together. We will set the fuse of these bombs with a very long delay so that the explosion will take place only after the bombs reach the bottom of the sea. It is clear to me that we'll have to conduct a test on our own nuclear submarine that would simulate the American vessel."

Colonel Yevgeni removed his glasses and wiped them thoroughly with his handkerchief.

"If the depth charges suit our purposes", said Yevgeni, placing his glasses back on his nose, "that will save a lot of time in preparing for the operation, as I assume that our Navy has a large variety of depth charges. Clearly it is preferable for us to conduct this operation from a Navy vessel that will lie in wait for the American submarine. It will facilitate everything and it will be much easier and simpler to execute the blast. If the Minister gives us his approval for this outline today, then we can fly to our large naval base in Murmansk tomorrow. With the letter that the Minister gave us, we will get everything that we ask for there and can deploy quickly for testing."

Brigadier General Dimitri raised his hand, requesting to speak.

"If we have already covered the subject of the blast, then, with your permission, Colonel Yevgeni, I would like to mention several things about the wireless communication with the submarines. Of course, it touches on the area of electronic warfare, and that's your baby, General Okhramenko."

The General nodded his acknowledgement, and Colonel Yevgeni motioned to Dimitri to continue.

"First of all, we must all know how wireless communication is conducted in submarines. Like everything in the military, this consists of three parts. At a shallow depth, let us say up to 20 meters underwater, the option is to release an inflatable with an antenna to float on the water's surface and to transmit and receive through it. Such an inflatable is almost out of use today, because it requires the submarine to reduce speed at a very shallow depth, making it visible and very vulnerable to a hit from the sea or from the air. In such a case, we should be ready with an appropriate communication block that will neutralize this inflatable. The maximum diving depth in training can be almost five hundred meters, which is about sixteen hundred feet. They conduct their navigation training at a depth of up to three hundred meters. At these depths, the Americans, like us, use an intricate network of underwater cables connected to hydrophones. These are transmitters and receivers which serve as relay stations for the submarines. This hydrophone network has two distinct advantages. One is high-quality communication, and the other is that the submarine does not reveal its location during the transmission. The big problem with this network, which is, in fact, our biggest advantage, is that the Americans, just like us, deploy such underwater networks only in areas that are near their territory and coasts. So when such a submarine arrives from the United States to the North Sea, for example, it is very far from the American underwater network and therefore cannot use it.

"The third possibility is the most practical one, and this is the method used by submarines when they are at medium to great depths. They use a frequency band called ELF, meaning extremely low frequency, 3 to

30 hertz. Do you understand? Not kilohertz and not megahertz but a few single hertz. Just so you fully comprehend, at these frequencies, the wavelength is between 10,000 to 100,000 kilometers. Do you get it? It's insane! But we can also understand that this is the only way for submarines at medium to great depths to communicate with their headquarters in the United States. Just to give you a sense of scale, we have reception antennas for these unique frequencies near the Murmansk Naval Base, and the Americans also have them in the Michigan area, and each of these antennas is more than 50 kilometers long. By the way, the submarines tow a huge metal cable underwater for this purpose, which serves them as an antenna."

Tea was served. Brigadier General Dimitri took a sip from his glass of tea and continued speaking.

"These frequencies - we must block them completely. That is the critical point of our entire plan", he said, and turned to the general. "General Okhramenko, how is this done? You probably know better than anyone."

The five team members awaited the words of the elderly general, but he said nothing, as though saying condescendingly, that's all? There is nothing simpler than this for me.

When his answer was late in coming, Colonel Yevgeni prodded him to speak and he finally deigned to reply.

"The description you provided, Mr. Brigadier General,

is correct, and I know it well. All the equipment and the instruments we need to execute communication blocks at all those frequencies are available, and are actually installed in quite a few of our large battleships. Therefore, I see no problem in carrying out the order."

Colonel Yevgeni gazed at the General, trying to decide whether his confidence in the proposed solution had any bearing. The General, one of the old school of Soviet generals, was bloated with self-importance, thought Yevgeni, but he probably knows what he is doing, not least because the Minister of Defense, the father of all ageing Soviet generals, introduced him as one of the greatest experts in the field of electronic warfare that the world had ever known.

"General Okhramenko", said Yevgeni. "I am very encouraged by your answer, but the last thing I want is a battleship in the region of the operation. Therefore, all the equipment and instruments that you referred to should quickly be installed on a civilian fishing boat that looks innocent. Only this vessel will be present in the perimeter of our operation and we shall conduct all our activities only from that."

Yevgeni glanced quickly at Brigadier General Dimitri, as if communicating a message.

"Comrades, it seems to me that tomorrow our behinds will already be in Murmansk. You, General Okhramenko, will have your work cut out for you there. Do we understand each other?"

The General continued displaying the same indifference, bordering on apathy, when he replied to Yevgeni as if in passing.

"The fishing boat should be of medium size or larger. I do not foresee a problem installing the equipment for the communication block, but some of the antennas are very large so a small vessel would present a problem. However, I have done much many complicated things in my life. We will find a solution."

Colonel Yevgeni looked again at the old white-haired general and wondered. Could my appointment as team leader, even though I am only a colonel, be causing the General to feel disrespected? Yevgeni tactically decided that there was no benefit in asking the General any further questions, and instead turned his attention to the Kazakh, Colonel Nazarbayev.

"You must take into account the fact that a fishing vessel will also know how to deploy the cluster of depth charges in the water."

"I don't see much of a problem with this, Colonel", the Kazakh replied readily. "Because if we take a medium-size or larger fishing boat, it is reasonable that it is also equipped with cranes large enough to do the job. Am I correct, Brigadier General Dimitri?

"Yes, you are correct, because these vessels lift nets with fish from the water and this is a large weight; but tomorrow we will be wiser and we will have all the data in our hands."

"Very well", said Colonel Nazarbayev. "I would like to continue discussing the method of introducing the depth charges into the water. Instead of hurling them from a catapult, as it is done on battleships, we will lower them into the water with the crane. In every case, their fuses will be set for a very long delay instead of less than half a minute, as with conventional charges. As it is now, and before we go into detail, we want the blast to occur on the seabed. As far as I know, and of course we will test this, the water depth in the North Sea or the Norwegian Sea may be more than two thousand meters. Therefore, the delay before the blast must be extremely long, and I hope that our navy has such fuses in its inventory. If not, we will improvise a device."

Yevgeni leaned back, drumming his fingers on the table.

"Very well. Thank you, everyone", he said, and glanced at his watch. "Lunch will be served soon, and then tomorrow, Marshal Budarenko will be coming. It seems to me that this time at least, we are more or less prepared to meet him, even though I really cannot guarantee the meeting's outcome."

Brigadier General Dimitri, on his right, tapped him affectionately on the shoulder and winked.

"Let's go smoke before lunch. You should practice your smoking, so your hands don't start shaking. Come, let's go."

CHAPTER 6

THE FRIENDSHIP AND MUTUAL RESPECT THAT HAD DEVELOPED between Brigadier General Dimitri and Colonel Yevgeni had already caused them to call each other by their first names and drop their military rank.

Dimitri leaned towards Yevgeni, who was sitting by his side, and whispered in his ear.

"I know that lady sitting by the Minister. She's the Head of Operations Research in the Navy, and is considered exceptionally gifted in her field."

Yevgeni nodded in reply.

The Minister of Defense ground his cigarette butt into the ashtray.

"I want to remind you that our primary plan for the invasion and occupation of the German Democratic Republic has already been approved by the Party's General Secretary, Vladimir Petrovich Yermolov. But that is only the beginning. All this vast force will be prepared and ready within three to four days and will be waiting, like a tightly coiled spring, only for you. We shall launch our Stage One of the military operation only after you succeed in creating for me the cause, the legitimacy, to continue from there directly to Stage B. Do you understand the responsibility that you bear and why we don't have any more time for fanciful suggestions?"

The Minister of Defense looked into the faces of the team members, all nervously awaiting his reaction, and that of his experts, to their plan.

"Colonel Yevgeni", the Minister thundered through his nicotine- thickened throat, "Speak up! What have you done today and what are you planning to do in the next two days?"

Yevgeni stood up and cleared his throat.

"Mr. Minister Marshal Budarenko. Today, we have already formed the plan and its details, and assigned tasks. Tomorrow, General Okhramenko, Brigadier General Dimitri, Colonel Nazarbayev and I will fly to Murmansk Naval Base and start working there."

"What exactly do you want to do in Murmansk?"

"We have several tasks there. The first task is to obtain a medium-size fishing boat that will be manned by our Navy seamen, and we shall install on it all the electronic equipment to block communication on the American submarine. The second mission is to conduct several tests with depth charges and survey the blast effects of a cluster of charges that we shall string together. We need to check their effectiveness when they explode on the sea bed, at a depth of several kilometers, and if they can even survive intact at such a depth. If the charges implode under the water pressure on their way down, we can reinforce their structure, or else we may have to use other ordnance."

Brigadier General Dimitri leaned toward Colonel Nazarba-yev, the explosives expert, and gently pulled the sleeve of his shirt.

"Both of us are stupid", Dimitri whispered to the Colonel. "Yevgeni is right. The bombs will implode under the water pressure way before they reach the sea bed. How did we not think of that? We are so lucky that Yevgeni has enough brains for all three of us."

The Minister turned to the woman on his right.

"This is your specialty. What do you have to say on the subject? Do you have any comments?"

The woman, about 35 years old, shifted her considerable frame in her chair. She wore a blue dress and her blond hair was worn in a long braid fastened at the back of her head in a very precise snail pattern.

"Colonel Yevgeni", the Operations Research specialist said quietly. "If you had consulted with Brigadier General Dimitri, I'm sure that he would have told you that the depth charges would be crushed at a depth of 500 to 600 meters. To go deeper than that, you need to reinforce the bombs in another steel shell, or maybe it is better if you search for another type of ordnance, maybe iron bombs, like those used by the Air Force. Of course, you will need to make some modifications."

The Minister of Defense shook his head incredulously, emphatically expressing his displeasure at what he had just heard.

"You have not even begun and your plan is already as full of holes as Swiss cheese", he said.

Just like the previous day, it was Colonel Yevgeni who volunteered to save the day by diverting the raging minister's wrath to himself.

"Mr. Minister Marshal Budarenko, this plan is a good plan, and I believe we will resolve the ordnance problem quite easily in Murmansk. For example, I've just had an idea that is worth looking into tomorrow. Our navy has round diving bells made of massive steel that are used for research. These bells are designed to be resistant to immense pressures at the greatest depths. I do not see a problem in fitting such a bell with a large amount of explosives and detonating it at the bottom of the sea."

Yevgeni finished his speech and looked at the Operations Research expert. Would she kill this idea that he had just pulled from up his sleeve, just to calm the Minister's mercurial temper? Or perhaps she would deem it appropriate and viable. The Minister was waiting for her response, but she weighed her words carefully before speaking.

"Mr. Minister, yes. I think it's definitely worth looking into."

The Minister shifted his gaze to Gregory, who all that time had been standing to attention by his side.

"Gregory, about tomorrow, have you already arranged their flight to Murmansk? Make sure that they receive the best treatment there, and get them out as soon as possible."

"Yes, sir", Gregory readily replied. "They are expected there tomorrow. There's a team there that has already started working on the requests and they have already found a fishing boat, and a full crew has been taken from a Navy supply ship. The crew will board the fishing boat tomorrow and prepare it for its mission."

The Minister's directions to Gregory made the think tank members realize that it was again Yevgeni, with his healthy common sense and creativity, who had saved them from another painful head-on collision with the Minister. This young man is a genius, pure genius, and exceptionally brave, thought Dimitri.

The Minister's loud voice boomed out again.

"Colonel Yevgeni will continue."

"Mr. Minister, I shall continue my briefing on the activity beginning tomorrow in Murmansk. After we install the equipment on the fishing boat and solve the issue with the bomb, we will sail out to sea with the submarine and conduct a full test. There are still two issues that we need to address thoroughly before the wet run at sea. Colonel Nazarbayev, together with other people, will have to finish all the preliminary computations that he needs to make regarding the precise location of the blast and the distance from the submarine. The second issue is that we don't have the American submarines' training schedule for the next few days. Naturally, this is essential so that we can lay in wait in the fishing boat for the submarine at the right place and at the right time.

"In fact, we know their navigation courses very well, as they haven't changed very much in the past few years. However, we don't have the precise timetable of these navigation exercises. Dimitri, excuse me, Brigadier General Dimitri, has already made contact with our people in Washington and they are very optimistic. They believe they can provide us with all the missing data within two days. These are the main issues, Mr. Minister."

Marshal Budarenko went into a short huddle with the woman at his side and with another man who had arrived with him, but who had not yet joined in the discussion. After their confidential exchange, the Minister turned back to the team.

"Now, assuming that the plan succeeds, though I still have my doubts", he said, "I want you, Colonel Yevgeni, to start outlining the outcomes and consequences of our operation."

"Mr. Minister, you mean how the American submarine will react after its captain is led to believe that the United States has been attacked by one or more nuclear missiles?" asked Yevgeni.

"Exactly."

"Mr. Minister, I propose that Brigadier General Dimitri present this scenario."

The Minister motioned impatiently with his hand as if saying, if you insist on Dimitri, then let it be Dimitri.

The Brigadier General stood up and approached the Minister and his retinue.

"If everything goes as planned and the American captain responds according to his orders", said Brigadier General Dimitri, "his submarine will then launch what they call the first portion of two or three nuclear missiles on the Soviet Union. The submarines are equipped with either

16 Poseidon missiles or 24 Trident missiles. After the launch of the first portion, the submarine Captain must wait for an order to launch the second salvo, but of course, in our case, this order will not arrive."

It was obvious that the Defense Minister did not like what he was hearing, and he was quick to cut Dimitri short.

"Wait a minute, stop. Do we know, or can we know, in which direction these two or three missiles, what you call an appetizer, will be launched?" the Minister of Defense asked.

"No, Mr. Minister. We have checked the issue thoroughly with our Washington people. It turns out that even this submarine Captain does not know where his missiles are aimed at. This is predetermined, and nobody in the submarine can interfere with the targets."

The Minister motioned restlessly at Dimitri, who stopped his presentation again. The Minister lit another cigarette and huddled again with his two experts.

"I understand the significance of being hit with several nuclear-tipped missiles", said the Minister. "On the other hand, I am actually encouraged that most of the 10,000 nuclear warheads that the Americans have are pre-assigned to targets, and I assume that most of the missiles are programmed to fall in our territory. So statistically, it is likely that the two or three missiles that we are hit with will not destroy our most important and highest-priority targets, out of the thousands of targets that the Americans have marked for destruction in case of all-out war. Furthermore, in the first stages of the war, I have no doubt that the Americans will not attack cities and population centers with nuclear weapons, except in response to such an act from us. It is most likely that their first target will be a heavy industry plant, an airport, or a seaport."

The Minister took another drag from his cigarette and leaned back to blow the smoke up towards the ceiling.

"What I want to say is, I can live with that", said the Minister after a pause. "Especially when the entire heavy industry of the German Federal Republic will fall intact into our hands during Stage B. This will be a pretty good compensation for the damage we will sustain from those two or three missiles."

It appeared that for the Minister of Defense, all this was just a game of chess on a wooden board. The Minister seemed to concern himself only with probable missile hits on the Soviet Union, assessing the damage that they could cause, without mentioning, even in one word, the casualties and panic that they could create. Thus, the minister concluded this scenario, with the laconic, chilling five-word sentence: "I can live with that."

CHAPTER 7

THREE HOURS HAD PASSED SINCE THE FIVE MEMBERS OF THE SPECIAL TEAM had boarded the Antonov 12 transport plane from Moscow to the northern port city of Murmansk. The loud, monotonous noise created by the plane's four turboprop engines all but prevented the team members from holding a conversation. Colonel Yevgeni had to shout into the ear of his colleague Brigadier General Dimitri.

"Can you hear me?"

"More or less. Talk loudly and slowly", Dimitri shouted back.

"You remember what we said about our sixth team member, the hard to identify fellow? His name is Vladimir, right?"

"Yes, Vladimir, from Military Intelligence, who is following our every move", Dimitri concurred.

"Exactly. Here is proof that we were right. We decided that the four of us would go - you, myself, Nazarbayev and the General - and suddenly we are five again."

"Yes, you're absolutely right. In fact, only Sergei, the Minister's assistant, isn't with us."

"We are taking a risk", said Yevgeni, "by conducting all the tests in Murmansk, of all places. It is our largest naval base and the closest to Western countries, and I'm sure that the

Americans focus their intelligence resources there and that Murmansk is constantly monitored."

"It makes sense, Yevgeni. But we don't have time to travel to the proving grounds on the other side of the country, like the one in Lensk, for example.

"Murmansk, for us, is like a huge supermarket. All you need to do is reach out to the shelf and take whatever you want. You want a fishing boat? You got it. You want a nuclear assault submarine? It's yours that same day. Over there in the East and at this time of year, the weather could shut us down for quite a few days. What would we do then? Do you think that you can make up another story for the Minister?" Dimitri asked.

Yevgeni did not answer, and Dimitri continued: "Maybe the Minister prefers us in the east because it is closer to the gulags of Siberia."

"Very funny", Yevgeni protested at Dimitri's grim joke.

After another hour of noisy travel, the wheels of the military transport plane hit the snow-lined tarmac of the airport near Murmansk. The city of Murmansk lies north of the Arctic Circle, not far from Finland's eastern border and on the coast of the Barents Sea, the northern waters of which were frozen already at this time of year.

A young officer, wearing a blue Navy uniform, greeted them as they disembarked from the plane. Wasting no time, he led them to two official black Lada cars parked, with engines running, next to the transport plane. Within half an hour, they had arrived at the massive iron gates of the large naval base. The younger officer exchanged a few words with the soldiers manning the checkpoint, and they were waved in through the gates, which opened to their full width. The official cars continued driving in the snow – it had been snowing nonstop before their arrival – until they stopped outside an isolated building at the center of the base. The young officer pointed towards the building.

"Rear Admiral Ilya Leonov, the Base Commandant, is expecting you here. Please follow me, officers."

The five team members and their escort walked up the wide staircase to the second floor of the building and into the well-heated office of the Commandant. Rear Admiral Leonov received them very warmly. Brigadier General Dimitri, the Navy man, was greeted with an embrace. The two had known each other for years.

Rear Admiral Leonov, at 55 years of age, seemed more like a senior official of the party than an old seaman. He was short in height and full in width and his blue Navy jacket was custom-tailored to accommodate his protruding belly. His hair was thin and white, and his cheeks were full and ruddy.

The office walls were paneled in a dark wood and covered with many photos of the Admiral, models of various naval vessels and unit insignia and coats of arms, marking the many high points of the Admiral's career. He invited his guests to sit at a table in a corner of the room. A seaman wearing the Navy dress uniform entered the room with a tray and placed it on the table. The tray held a variety of sandwiches, but above all, a steaming tea kettle.

"How was the flight?" asked Rear Admiral Leonov.

"Noisy and tiring", Dimitri replied without elaborating.

"We have prepared a meal for you in the senior officers' residence. The conditions there are excellent. You can rest there for a while and freshen up, and tomorrow you will be as good as new", the Admiral said, looking round at his guests.

"Your liaison Gregory sent me a full list of your requests for personnel and equipment", he continued, "and all is already prepared and ready for you. To accommodate your request, I've cancelled a scheduled exercise for one of our most advanced submarines, which was due to leave tomorrow. From tomorrow, this submarine and its crew are under your command. Shall we meet in the morning, then?"

Yevgeni answered for the team.

"Sir, as the head of the team, I would like to thank you for your hospitality and for your swift and efficient preparations for us."

"Hold on, Colonel", the Admiral interrupted him, shifting his gaze again and again from Yevgeni to Dimitri to General Okhramenko. "I want to understand; you are a colonel, right?"

"True."

Yevgeni already understood where his host was heading with his question.

"So how is it that you are heading a team which includes a General and a Brigadier General?"

Brigadier General Dimitri, the Admiral's friend, put his hand on Yevgeni's shoulder as if to tell him, please leave this matter to me.

"This is a very special team", said Dimitri, "and this Yevgeni is simply a genius. Every time we reached a dead end, he was the only one who knew how to get us all out of it and continue in a new direction. Even Marshal Budarenko, of all people, was impressed by his fantastic abilities, and that is why he appointed Yevgeni to lead the team."

Rear Admiral Leonov was still perplexed, but finally said, "If Marshal Budarenko so decided, then I have no doubt that he made the best decision for all of you. You, Colonel, couldn't receive a better compliment than this."

Colonel Yevgeni thanked the Admiral with a slight bow of the head and decided to cut short the small talk and to get to the reason for their being there.

"Rear Admiral Leonov, I understand that you were requested to designate for us three teams of the best of your people in order for us to start work immediately."

"That's right", replied the Rear Admiral. "We've put together three teams, and all of them are already here at the base. The first team is made up of explosives and sea ordnance specialists. The second is made up of experts in communications and electronic warfare, and the third includes operations research specialists and math prodigies, or something like that. Tomorrow morning you will meet all of them."

"Excellent", Yevgeni replied curtly. "But I have something to ask of you. I apologize that we are not allowed to disclose the subject that we are dealing with at the moment, but to have a good night's sleep, or even to have a rest, is a luxury we cannot afford. We are under supervision, and Marshal Budarenko is watching us now from Moscow, and we shouldn't be surprised if he suddenly lands here with no prior notice. I want to meet with the three teams now. Each of us will work with his relevant team until we get answers and make progress, even if it continues throughout the night. Therefore, can you please call your teams to work now, maybe in a few minutes?"

The Admiral's expression made it clear that he was still dissatisfied, if not annoyed, by Yevgeni, that thin, strange-looking Colonel. The Admiral was still trying to understand how the Colonel, who did not even look like a military officer, was dispensing orders to a General, and especially to a General of the old school. Moreover, it seemed to him that the Colonel did not even appreciate the Admiral's hospitality and the great resources that he was allocating to the unprepossessing Colonel on the vast naval base over which he ruled like a demigod. However, since the Colonel had come on a mission on behalf of Marshal Budarenko, and under his direct orders, the Admiral understood that he would do well to overlook the bad manners and keep his cool, and especially his head, and do exactly as instructed by the Colonel. He lifted his heavy figure from his seat, went to his desk and pressed the intercom button. He was answered by the voice of a young man. The senior naval officer shot a string of short orders into the intercom and returned to his guests.

Notwithstanding the urgency, Dimitri exchanged niceties and small talk with the Admiral for a few minutes, asking after his family, his wife and two sons.

The intercom emitted a discordant buzzing sound. The Admiral pushed the blinking button and increased the sound volume on the box.

"Yes", he replied sharply.

"Sir, I was informed that most of the personnel have been located and they will wait for you in 15 minutes' time in the main conference room at Naval Intelligence."

Colonel Yevgeni turned to his friend Dimitri and whispered in his ear.

"I thank you for the knowledgeable explanation you gave the Admiral. Next time we raise the subject, please ask our friend the General to explain." Yevgeni leaned back in his chair and winked at Dimitri.

The five left the Admiral to meet the three work teams that were already waiting for them. As they were walking in the snow, which had been falling since they arrived at the base,

Dimitri clutched Yevgeni's arm.

"Yevgeni, I hope you're not taking the compliments that I am making up about you too seriously. The last thing I want is for you to start believing my lies."

"Yes, I've already got that", Yevgeni said sardonically. "By the way, Brigadier General, as my personal attendant, you were derelict in your duty to light me a cigarette every hour on the hour. Is my health not important to you anymore?"

The Naval Intelligence building was surrounded by a tall wire fence. At the entrance gate, a naval lieutenant greeted them with a salute. According to his chest insignia, he was a submariner. He led them inside and gave them a short tour.

"Good evening, gentlemen. My name is Alexey Buchenko, and I will be attached to you 24 hours a day. I will coordinate everything that you require here on the base. Here, in this building, you can work under the best conditions. This building is compartmentalized externally and internally. Your accommodations are here, just across the room. By the way, your luggage has already been distributed in the rooms. Please follow me."

As they walked in, Brigadier General Dimitri turned to Alexey.

"Lieutenant Alexey, on which submarine are you serving?"

"K-219, Navaga Class, Brigadier General."

The young submarine officer felt great pride when he named the nuclear assault submarine that he was serving on, which was state of the art and the pride of the submarine fleet.

Colonel Yevgeni was the first to enter the conference room on the second floor of the Intelligence building. The room contained some 15 officers, men and women, and they all rose to attention in unison as Marshal Budarenko's special team entered the room. They continued to stand as Yevgeni and his other team members took their seats at the conference table. Yevgeni motioned to them to be seated.

"Good evening, everyone", he said.

"Good evening, Colonel", the teams replied, almost in unison.

"We have a shared mission of the utmost importance to our Armed Forces and to the Soviet Union, and we shall execute it as well and as quickly as possible. That is why you were brought here without delay. We shall now split up into three teams, and each team will be joined by one of my men. Because there is a need for continuous communication between the teams, the most efficient way is for all three teams to be working in the same room. Therefore, we shall split up into three groups here in this room. The ordnance and explosives team will assemble in the left-hand corner of the room. You will be led and guided by Colonel Nazarbayev", Yevgeni said, pointing to the Kazakh Colonel.

"Those of you in the communications and electronic warfare team will get together in the right-hand corner. You will be headed by General Okhramenko."

Yevgeni placed his hand on the General's shoulder in a gesture that seemed patronizing to most of those present, coming from an officer of an inferior rank.

"The third team is made up of the operations research and mathematics specialists. Please come here; you will be working with me. The two remaining members of our team will alternate between the teams. Let's go!"

Yevgeni watched the obedient naval officers carry out his instructions without comment – each man and woman walked to his or her position. He now examined, with great interest, the three male and the two female officers around him. Yevgeni turned to the most senior, a female Lieutenant Commander.

"I understand that you received a preliminary briefing this morning. Is this correct? And by the way, what is your name?"

"My name, Sir, is Lieutenant Commander Doctor Irena Pashutin, and my doctorate is in operations research. And yes, Sir, we were indeed briefed this morning."

"Very well. Is one of you a seismologist, as I requested?"

A young junior Lieutenant raised his hand.

"I am, Sir. My name is Lieutenant Junior Grade Belov."

Yevgeni scanned the faces of the other team members, but decided that this was not the time to elaborate on their functions, preferring to get to work immediately.

"Your mission is perhaps the easiest and the shortest, but it also requires the most precision. Your starting point for all your calculations is a nuclear blast with a magnitude of twenty megatons. You should calculate for me what the earthquake value should be, or the magnitude of a land shockwave on the Richter scale that is felt at a distance of six thousand nautical miles from the blast's epicenter. That is essentially your job as a seismologist, Lieutenant Junior Grade Belov. This is where we'll start, your starting point. This point, which, as I said, is six thousand nautical miles from the explosion, we shall name the Alpha Point. The magnitude of the shockwave that we get at Alpha Point, which will be measured on the Richter scale, we shall call R. Is everything clear so far?"

The five officers concurred, nodding their heads.

"Now we advance to the next stage. I want to create a small explosion, using standard explosives, not far from that Alpha Point. The explosion must be made under two conditions.

One, the explosion will take place far enough away from our Alpha Point that acoustically, the explosion will not be heard at Alpha Point. The second condition is that the magnitude of the blast, the same R value, identical to that received from a nuclear explosion far away, will be received at Alpha Point. What we need to find out is how many kilos of standard army explosive, and at what distance from Alpha Point, would create that blast. Will two hundred kilos of TNT at a distance of 10 kilometers from Alpha create the desired effect, or perhaps I need to explode half a ton of TNT thirty kilometers away from Alpha? This is exactly what I need to get from you."

Yevgeni finished his speech and looked at the five officers sitting across from him. It seems, he thought, that I am not really challenging them. He would now challenge them with another task, and maybe then they would start sweating.

"So far things are simple and relatively easy. Right, Lieutenant Colonel Doctor Pashutin?"

"Yes, Sir", answered the operations research specialist. "This is really not complicated and you will get exactly the two figures that you requested. However, Colonel, you probably intend to carry out the blast at a specific location. Therefore, I need to get data on the type of soil at that location. I also need to know the temperature and wind speeds and directions at that location. These are important for our calculations. Of course, I mean the data for the two regions, points, Alpha and R."

Yevgeni decided that now was the time to give the team a shot of motivation, before elaborating on their mission.

"Before we left Moscow to come here, I asked for a team made up of the best of the best in the Soviet Union. I am happy to see that this is exactly the case."

"Thank you, Colonel, for the compliment", replied Dr. Pashutin. Yevgeni hurried back to his subject.

"Everything you said is very true, but I can't provide some of what you requested, for reasons of state security. Moreover, we are now coming to another stage where the picture gets a little more complicated."

The officers, three men and two women, listened closely to what the colonel had to say, and were even more attentive than before.

"The speed of sound in the air is well known, even to schoolchildren. In water, however, the speed of the sound waves is about three times faster. I am reminding you of this because our Alpha Point is actually located 300 meters underwater."

"Then it is a submarine!" exclaimed Doctor Pashutin almost involuntarily, as if she were a schoolgirl.

"Exactly", replied Yevgeni. "We do not need soil data. Please consider the sea and climate data that are prevalent and typical during this season here, in the sea near Murmansk."

Yevgeni again paused for a few seconds, to give his words more emphasis.

"In light of this new data, your answer as to the size of the explosive charge and distance must contain another critical piece of information. In order to obtain the same result, which we are calling R, with our Alpha Point being underwater, should the explosion take place above water, or perhaps on the water surface, or even on the sea bed, which is two thousand meters deep at that point?"

Yevgeni stood up and motioned to the group of officers to remain seated, as they were about to rise to their feet in respect.

"Before I move on to the other teams, please tell me if everything is clear. Do you have any questions to ask me?" Yevgeni asked.

"Everything is clear, Colonel", Dr. Pashutin replied.

"And when do you estimate I will have your answers?" asked Yevgeni.

"We need to collect historical data stored in various seismic stations, and all the rest is already available to us. There is a chance that we can provide you with data before daybreak", replied Dr. Pashutin.

"Very well", Yevgeni said. "I'll be staying here in the room, and if you need clarifications or more data, please do not hesitate to ask."

Brigadier general Dimitri approached Yevgeni and asked, "Have you made progress with your geniuses?"

"It appears that they really are geniuses, especially the female officer, the Lieutenant Commander Doctor. She has a doctorate in operations research, she is sharp, she understands the mission, and I think their part will be finished before daybreak."

"Sounds great", replied Dimitri.

"Now look, we have another issue, of field security, or counter- intelligence, that may belong to our anonymous team member, the KGB man. But I believe it falls under your overall responsibility and authority", said Yevgeni.

"What is the problem? What field security?"

"I had to tell the mathematics genius team that the center of activity is a submarine, and that they should take that into account. I think it is better that you remind your friend, the Admiral, of the letter from the Minister of Defense, and instruct him that all three team members must immediately be placed in total isolation. In my opinion, this is essential until our operation is concluded. What do you say?"

"I think you are right. By the way, I wouldn't be surprised if he's already received such an order, but I will still tell him. Come, let's check the other teams. Let's see how our sensitive fellow the General, Okhramenko, is doing."

The two joined the General and the local team attached to him. The

General's face expressed his characteristic smugness now that he had people under his command who were making progress, and Yevgeni decided to check if it was justified.

"General Okhramenko, how are we doing? Are there any problems?"

The General looked at Yevgeni dismissively, as if he were asking how he liked his tea.

"Oh, there is no problem", the General finally said. "Just as I already told you in Moscow. The officers here have already instructed the technical section in the shipyard to dismantle several instruments and antennas from one of the frigates that are moored here, and tomorrow in daylight they can be installed on the trawler."

"More power to you, General. Can I move on, then?" Yevgeni asked, somewhat sarcastically.

"You are dismissed", the General said, and Yevgeni pretended not to hear.

Yevgeni and Dimitri then joined Colonel Nazarbayev's team. In the past few days, the two had come to like him and to share with him the closeness and fondness that they felt towards each other. They especially liked his sincerity and modesty.

"How goes it in your kingdom, Comrade Colonel?' Yevgeni asked.

"It isn't straightforward", replied Nazarbayev. "We are trying to think of applicable solutions."

"And where is the main problem?"

"The depth charges have been completely ruled out", said the explosives expert. "Indeed, I am sitting here with the best experts. The depth charges are built just like ordinary barrels, and at a depth of several hundred meters, they will be crushed. We contacted an aerial ordnance specialist, and we are checking the possibility of dropping an aerial bomb from a jet fighter-bomber. Because of the aerodynamic structure of the aerial bomb, it will enter the water at a very high speed. The problem will be the bomb's fuse. Delaying the explosion until the bomb reaches the bottom of the sea is no problem, but as it looks now, the challenge that we are facing is that the fuse of the aerial bomb can jam because water will seep into it under extreme atmospheric pressure. The solution will have to come from improvisation."

Colonel Yevgeni scratched his head and looked with concern at his teammate and buddy Dimitri, who was thinking about Nazarbayev's problem.

"I would like to tell you, my friend, Colonel Nazarbayev, that you're absolutely right and we need to think of an improvisation, especially since we only have to meet a one-time need. Our solution does not have to comply with the standards of manufacturing a series of such bombs. I will tell you a story, and maybe your teammates should also hear it."

Colonel Nazarbayev turned to call his five teammates, but there was no need for that as they had already been following the conversation with interest.

"They are listening. Please go on, Colonel Yevgeni."

"Well, this is the story. Once upon a time in a war, and I don't remember exactly which one, maybe the Great Patriotic War. It's a true story of an extraordinary capacity for improvisation. One of our Air Force planes discovered during the fighting that the bombs they dropped on enemy ships pierced through the ships before exploding. In other words, the bombs went clean through the ships, continued sinking and only then went off, underwater. To solve the problem, they needed another type of fuse with a shorter delay, so that the bombs would only penetrate the upper deck and go off inside the ship. You realize that such an explosion inside a ship is the most effective way to sink it, and that the ship has almost no chance of surviving.

"Of course, the middle of a war is not the best time for developing and manufacturing new fuses, as this can take a year or even more. Everybody tried to come up with a solution, until one junior ordnance officer from one of the bomber squadrons came up and proposed an idea that, superficially, sounded dumb, if not totally weird. But then someone in the system decided to check it out anyway. The outcome was that the enemy ships started sinking one by one."

Yevgeni felt like a teacher in front of young students, who were all agog and curious to hear the end of the story.

"The junior officer", Yevgeni continued, "proposed to use standard impact fuses, which go off immediately upon impact, and to put into them one half of a wooden laundry clip. With a wooden clip in the fuse, when the bomb hit the target, it required another fraction of a second for the clip to be crushed and for the fuse to detonate the bomb. This way, the blast happened after the bomb pierced the upper deck and was already inside the ship."

Yevgeni looked at the smiling faces of the team members. "That's a good story, right?"

The ordnance team agreed, waiting for more.

"Now, you're asking yourselves why I told you the story, right? Well, the reason is not what you think, to encourage you to think of an improvisation or something new. I just wanted to gain a few more minutes so I can also come up with an idea."

The team members smiled. This time, and in light of Colonel Yevgeni's openness and humor, some of the ordnance team members felt free to laugh openly.

"Which one of you knows best about depth charges?" Yevgeni asked, and one naval officer, a Lieutenant raised his hand and stood up.

"Sir, Lieutenant Ilya Trepishchev, Commandant of the Undersea Ordnance Section."

Yevgeni waved the Lieutenant back to his seat.

"Lieutenant Trepishchev, the fuses of the depth charges are watertight. I am considering the possibility of fitting such a fuse to an aerial bomb. If the fuse cannot withstand the high pressure at the seabed, maybe it can be protected by a steel cone, like a hat, that we can weld to the nose of the bomb in a way that will also preserve the bomb's aerodynamic quality. We will only extend it by several centimeters. It seems simple to me because these bombs are made of iron."

Lieutenant Trepishchev looked at Yevgeni, requesting permission to reply.

"Speak up, Lieutenant. I'm listening."

"In principle, it is possible, but it depends on the diameter of the screw thread of the nose bearing shell. If the thread of the aerial bomb's fuse is larger, I can very easily make an adapter that will allow the bomb charge's fuse to fit into the aerial bomb. It's simple to make such an adapter", the Major said.

"Please tell me, Lieutenant, what happens if it's the other way around, meaning the fuse of the charge is thicker and fatter than the screw thread in the aerial bomb? What do you do then?"

The lieutenant seemed to choose his words carefully and then, with a slight smile, he said: "Then, Colonel, we would have a real problem. I think we may have to find that junior officer who used laundry clips in bombs."

The Lieutenant immediately regretted using a type of language that was unacceptable in such military forums. To his great surprise and relief, he noticed that Yevgeni was smiling.

This fellow is either rude or he is very brave, thought Yevgeni, and he is exactly the type of person that can make a difference when necessary.

IT WAS WAY PAST MIDNIGHT WHEN YEVGENI RETURNED TO his first team, the operations researchers. When Dr. Irena Pashutin noticed him, she stopped working on the paperwork laid out before her.

"Well, have you reached a solution?" asked Yevgeni. "Yes, Sir Colonel", Pashutin replied.

Yevgeni called over his four teammates and all of them waited patiently for Dr. Pashutin's explanation.

"We have completed all the calculations and validated the data several times", said Dr. Pashutin. "In order to produce the R effect that will optimally simulate a nuclear blast, which will allegedly occur at a distance of six thousand nautical miles, we need to detonate approximately 500 kilograms of standard issue Red Army explosives at a distance of 47 kilometers from Alpha Point."

"What is the Alpha Point?" Colonel Nazarbayev asked.

Yevgeni motioned swiftly to Dr. Pashutin to disregard the question, saying to his mate Nazarbayev, "I'll explain to you later"; then he turned back to Dr. Pashutin.

"Lieutenant Commander Doctor, what is the most effective location to execute the blast? Is it over water? At the water surface level, on the seabed, or somewhere in between? Have you reached a decision on this?"

"Yes, Sir", replied Dr. Pashutin. "I am sorry I did not say this before, but the most effective blast, compatible with the data you provided, Colonel, should be conducted on the seabed."

Lieutenant Alexey, the young submarine officer, entered the room. He saluted Yevgeni and informed him that a meal was ready for them in the next room. Yevgeni saluted him back and thanked him, and the younger officer quickly left the room. Yevgeni announced a half-hour break, but requested that his four colleagues remain with him for an inter-team coordination session.

"The fog is starting to clear", said Yevgeni. "In my opinion, within 24 hours, we can go out to sea for a full wet run. Colonel Nazarbayev, excuse me for not keeping you up-to-date. The Alpha Point is where the American submarine will be cruising at the time of the blast. General Okhramenko, I understand that tomorrow, installations and fittings on the trawler will be completed. Am I right?"

"Right, Colonel", the General replied curtly.

"Colonel Nazarbayev", Yevgeni said. "We now understand that we need to deliver 500 kilos of explosive to the bottom of the sea. With these numbers, our situation is not so bad, because a standard 1-ton aerial bomb contains about 500 kilos of explosive, while the other 500 kilos are its metal components. I ask that you immediately activate whoever needs to be activated in order to fly two one-thousand- kilogram bombs from the nearest Air Force base. Actually, not two but three. The bombs must be here by morning. Is that clear?"

"Yes, Colonel Yevgeni", Colonel Nazarbayev answered.

"By the way", Yevgeni continued, "I don't want any fighter jet to drop a bomb for me in the sea. I have two good reasons for that. One, I don't want the Americans to detect any aerial activity in the perimeter of our operation. Two, I'm afraid that when the bomb hits the water with force, its non-standard, improvised fuse will be damaged, if not activated. Therefore, we will do it differently. We will do it like a couple of hedgehogs making love – very, very carefully."

The team members, including the dour General, broke into relieved laughter, all of them feeling that they had indeed made substantial ground that evening. When they resumed their serious expressions, Yevgeni continued.

"We will drop the bomb from the trawler using a crane. The bomb is very heavy, but with its elegant aerodynamic figure, it will sink quickly to the seabed. What do you say, my friend, Colonel Nazarbayev?"

"What I am saying", Nazarbayev said with amusement, "is that I am starting to get tired of agreeing with you all the time. But it sounds logical to me."

"Excellent, and now you, Brigadier General Dimitri. It seems to me that by tomorrow, we can complete all the preparations, and the day after tomorrow, we can go out to sea for the test. I'm reminding you that we are almost ready, in theory, and we have only one missing detail, which seems marginal but is not. We have no target. We have no American vessel on which to execute all this giant operation. We still don't have a training and navigation schedule for the American submarines."

Dimitri glanced at his watch and calculated for a minute before turning to Yevgeni.

"Look, it is already one past midnight, but I am going to find and wake Admiral Leonov. Only he would have a secure telephone that can connect us to our people in Washington. They promised us results within a day or two, but I want to put pressure on them."

Brigadier General Dimitri stood up and walked towards the door.

"One more thing, Dimitri", Yevgeni called to him. "Tell your friend that we will meet him tomorrow at 0800 hours for an important conference. Tell him that we want the naval captain of the trawler and also the captain of the nuclear submarine with him at the meeting, as they will also join us in the experiment. We are nearing the end of our work tonight. Let's eat something and meet up at the residence."

Colonel Nazarbayev rose to his feet and walked towards the door. Yevgeni's eyes followed him.

"Where are you going?"

"I am not one hundred percent certain of everything. I want to go with the local team to their section and check a few things for myself. I will join you later. Good night, dear colleagues, or should I say, good morning to you."

CHAPTER 8

REAR ADMIRAL ILLYA LEONOV INVITED HIS GUESTS TO SIT with him around the desk in his office. He poured steaming hot tea from a glass teapot for himself, and urged his guests to do the same.

"Did my people come up with the goods last night?" he asked, expecting only one answer.

Colonel Yevgeni placed his cup of tea on the table.

"I have nothing but compliments for you and your people. They truly are first-class professionals."

The Admiral was pleased, but then folded his arms across his chest and looked severe.

"I understand that you are going to blow up the whole port here." "What do you mean?" Yevgeni protested.

"I mean", said the Admiral, "that late last night or early this morning, a truck entered my base with three one-ton bombs aboard. No one was kind enough to warn me in advance."

Although the most senior naval officer spoke in a calm voice, Yevgeni did not need his sharp senses to understand that the Admiral was angry, that he was exercising his rank and responsibility, and that his words were a sharp rebuke.

"I apologize, Sir", Yevgeni replied. "You are correct. I should have notified you, but I didn't feel comfortable waking you up in the middle of the night."

"These are Air Force aerial bombs. What exactly do you intend to do with them, with my people? I don't have planes here, and our naval Kamov helicopters can't lift anything like one of these bombs."

"You are right", Yevgeni replied. "We're going to install a waterproof naval fuse in one of those bombs and then try to drop the bomb into the sea using the trawler's crane. By the way, speaking of the trawler, I requested that this meeting be attended by its captain and also by the captain of the submarine that we are collaborating with. Where are they?"

"They will join us in a few minutes. I wanted to have a few minutes with you alone here first."

Brigadier General Dimitri, the Rear Admiral's old friend, now spoke.

"My friend Rear Admiral Leonov. As we are your guests on this base, it is my duty to inform you of all our plans for today and also for tomorrow."

"Only guests?" replied the Admiral in a commanding tone, "Not once in my long life of service to the Soviet Union have I had 'guests'", – the Admiral pronounced the word *guests* emphatically to sound almost like *invaders* – "who arrived with a letter from the Minister of Defense that states that I have no discretion and I must provide them with anything and everything they ask for. I wanted to understand, I am not complaining. It's obvious that the Minister would have not given you such a letter had it not been of the utmost importance, but to be honest, this is the first time I have encountered such a situation."

No one answered, and the Admiral concluded: "Well, it doesn't matter. Go on Dimitri, go on."

Dimitri preferred not to discuss the issue that the Admiral had raised, justifiably, in his opinion, which actually contravened all known standing orders. The Admiral was graceful enough for someone in his position, so Dimitri continued talking technicalities.

"Today we will work in the pier area of the port. We will board the trawler, study it, and get to know its crew. General Okhramenko will make sure that the electronic warfare equipment is installed correctly and effectively on this fishing vessel. The operators of this equipment must connect the equipment and coordinate with the boat crew. Most of the work will be done in the ordnance section, and that's why Colonel Nazarbayev is not here with us. He is already in the section with your officers, and I hope that by the end of the day they will be ready to go out to sea tomorrow."

"And what are you planning for tomorrow?" asked the Admiral.

"Tomorrow morning we will sail aboard the trawler to the area of your firing range. I understand it is about thirty miles from the shoreline."

"Correct", the Admiral confirmed.

"When we arrive there, we will perform a test drop of the bomb, with the hope that it will require no further testing."

"You also requested a submarine, and not just any ordinary submarine but one of our most advanced. What is its part in this?" the Admiral inquired.

"Colonel Yevgeni and I will be on the submarine, and it will sail to a precise location that we will specify. At that point, the submarine will collect data of the blast, and General Okhramenko's team, on the trawler, will try to shut down the eyes and ears of the submarine. In general, that is the full outline of what we are doing."

Someone knocked at the door of the Admiral's office, and Lieutenant Alexey, the young submarine officer, entered. Behind him were two naval officers. The Admiral motioned to them to enter, and the Lieutenant walked several steps, came to a stop, snapped to attention and saluted. The other two officers remained at the door.

"Sir, I have with me Captain Lev Yashin and Commander Vitaly Dobrinin, Sir."

"Come, gentlemen, join us", Rear Admiral Leonov said, his eyes on the junior submariner officer, who remained at attention.

"You are relieved, Lieutenant", he said.

"Sorry, Sir. I have here an envelope to deliver personally to Brigadier

General Dimitri", said the Lieutenant. The Admiral pointed at Dimitri.

"Here he is. You can give it to him now."

Lieutenant Alexey removed a brown paper envelope sealed with red wax from under his arm. Dimitri signed a form that Alexey gave him, returned it to him, opened the envelope, glanced at it and quickly closed it.

"Good news", Dimitri whispered to Yevgeni who sat by his side, "We have it. This is from my conversation last tonight with our friends across the ocean."

Yevgeni nodded in satisfaction.

Rear Admiral Leonov introduced the two naval captains, who took their seats at the table. He turned to the trawler's new captain.

"There's only one other team member who will be aboard the trawler tomorrow", the Admiral told the Major. "His name is Colonel Nazar... never mind. By the way, is he Uzbek or Kazakh?"

Brigadier General Dimitri could not hide his amusement at his friend's excessive interest in the ethnic background of his Kazakh Colonel friend.

"His name is Nazarbayev and he is a Kazakh by birth. He is a top officer, the best of the best", Dimitri said.

"All right, Kazakh", the Admiral responded with a smile, and turned again to the two officers who had just joined them.

"Our colleagues have come from Moscow and we are ordered to fulfill all their needs and requests. Let's start with you, Commander. What is the status of your new vessel?"

The Admiral pointed to Commander Vitaly. "Of course, he is the fisherman", he added in a disparaging tone.

Vitaly looked like a typical Russian. His face was round and fair and his eyes were blue. He seemed about 50 years old and his blonde hair was well cropped. He was average in stature with broad shoulders, and his navy blue uniform seemed somewhat worn and unkempt.

"We have already spent thirty-six hours on the trawler", said Commander Vitaly. "I have twenty-three seamen and four officers on board. They took their positions quickly and are in control, as our supply ship and this fishing vessel are quite similar. In general, the trawler is in well maintained, and it is now being equipped with military communication equipment. Another crew, that I assume is related to you, is installing electronic equipment, of which I don't know many details."

"Better that you don't know", General Okhramenko said dryly. This was the first time he had spoken at the meeting.

"By the way, how far can the cranes extend beyond the deck

and how much can they lift?" Colonel Yevgeni asked.

"In general", Commander Vitaly said, leafing through some papers, "The ship has very powerful cranes, as they need to lift fishing nets with huge amounts of fish from the sea. Here is the data. We have two large cranes, one on the stern and one on the bow, with a lifting capacity of up to four and a half tons each, and there are two more, one on the portside and one on the starboard, with a lifting capacity of three tons each. Regarding the length of the arms, I..."

Dimitri interrupted the commander.

"It doesn't matter now. There are two more things that that I need from you, Commander. Tonight, we will be loading a bomb weighing one ton onto your ship. Also, we are sending several ordnance personnel and operators of electronic equipment on board your ship. Eight men in total, who are actually the most important people in all our maneuvers. Now, the most important thing for you to do is to return quickly to your ship and personally supervise all the preparations, as tomorrow at 0800 hours we set out to sea, to the area of your naval range."

"We will be ready and on time, Colonel. Am I dismissed?" asked the commander.

"Yes, Commander", replied his direct commanding officer, the Admiral.

While Commander Vitaly was making his way towards the door, Rear Admiral Ilya Leonov tapped Captain Yashin's shoulder with his hand.

"Gentlemen, this is Captain Yashin, commander of Nuclear Assault Submarine K-219, Navaga class. The Captain is one of the best sons of our beloved Soviet Union."

The Captain looked about 40 years old, handsome, with a

narrow face and blond hair combed back. He had an athletic build and his navy blue uniform gave him a distinguished look. He chose not to respond to the compliments he had just received, and remained seated in his chair, upright and silent.

As the person closest to the submarine commander's occupation, it was only natural that Dimitri was the one to start a conversation with him.

"Captain Yashin, your mission will be quite simple, because it is largely passive. Tomorrow, at 0800 hours, some of our people will be sailing out aboard the trawler to a firing range that you know. When they are ready to execute the test there, your submarine will be exactly 47 kilometers north of them. Of course, you will receive a precise location point."

Dimitri again opened the brown envelope, and removed the contents that he had glanced at only a few minutes earlier.

"Please excuse me for a moment ", he said.

He stepped aside, going through the papers which he held on his knees and, a few minutes time later, he put the papers back in the envelope and rejoined the group.

"Back to our subject; your submarine will be at the same location at a depth of two hundred and ninety meters exactly. Colonel Yevgeni and I will join you aboard your vessel There is no need for any special equipment or any particular specialist, as your full regular crew is sufficient for this mission and we will be working with them. Is everything clear, Captain?"

The submarine commander nodded and pulled his shoulders back.

"There is nothing to understand, Colonel. You are asking us to do nothing", replied the submarine commander.

"This is true", Dimitri said. "It may be said that I need your submarine almost as inert metal at the right place, at the right time and at the right depth, but its presence there is crucial to the mission. Colonel Yevgeni and I cannot operate this monster all by ourselves. But I have something else to tell you, Captain Yashin, something very important. Nobody in the submarine, but nobody, should know that there is a vessel in the perimeter of the range or that their submarine is involved in any kind of test. We must check and see if, and what, your operators aboard the submarine discover about an explosion taking place in their range, but without them knowing anything of this ahead of time. This is a critical point, and this alone will determine if the test is successful or if it is a waste of time and resources. Please inform everyone from your deputy down that we are guests from Moscow, from the Ministry of Defense, or you can tell them that we are tourists, or you can tell them anything. That's it as far as tomorrow. Is everything clear so far?"

Captain Yashin nodded.

"From tomorrow", Dimitri continued, "After we return, your submarine will not sail anywhere. It will remain here at the port on a sea-mission alert, with a six-hour advance notice. At the moment, I cannot tell you how long it will last. On the day that we sail out to our operation, your submarine will escort the trawler. You will follow it by periscope. Before going out to sea, you will receive an envelope from me with another top secret mission. You will be allowed to unseal this envelope only after our trawler reaches its destination and drops anchor there. That's all, Captain. We'll see you tomorrow morning."

The submarine commander rose up, bowed his head slightly to the Admiral, and hurried out the door. Yevgeni looked at Dimitri and smiled ironically.

"What's so funny?" Dimitri asked.

"I don't think you'll end up as good friends, you and the submarine commander. No matter, the most important is that we'll be in good hands tomorrow. Say, maybe you should go alone? It simply doesn't seem natural to me to enter an iron pipe and even dive in it. It may be more suitable for unhealthy people, I mean, not right in the head. Well, I think we've exhausted the subject. Let's go visit our Kazakh friend. That poor fellow hasn't had a second of sleep in forty-eight hours."

"Thank you, Rear Admiral Leonov", Yevgeni said.

"The best of luck, Colonel", the Admiral said, remaining at his desk, and the four team members left the room.

LIEUTENANT ALEXEY LED THE FOUR TEAM MEMBERS ON the paths leading to the vast hangars of the ordnance section, where they were to meet Colonel Nazarbayev. Yevgeni stopped the group near a small and derelict-looking hangar. He opened its door and looked inside.

"Follow me", he called out to his teammates. "Lieutenant Alexey, please remain out here. Make sure that no one disturbs us." "Will do, Sir", Alexey replied.

Predictably, it was Vladimir, whom Yevgeni and Dimitri had dubbed "the sixth fellow", who must secretly represent military intelligence, who first questioned Yevgeni.

"Colonel Yevgeni, what are you doing?" "Follow me and you'll all see", replied Yevgeni.

The four walked into a small hall that looked like a welding workshop. In the center of the workshop stood an iron table with remnants of sheet metal and iron bars. Yevgeni motioned to his friends to join him around the table.

"Dimitri", Yevgeni said, "you can open the envelope here. The contents of this envelope are the heart of the matter, and here we can assume that there are no hidden microphones or cameras and that nothing will leak out. Do you understand me now, Vladimir, my friend?"

Vladimir watched Yevgeni without expression and did not say a word.

Dimitri opened the envelope which, to his teammates' surprise, contained only two pages appearing at first glance, to be photocopies of documents taken under less than optimal conditions. At the top of each page, the U.S. Navy emblem was printed, and in each center, a golden eagle, with its wings spread, held an anchor in its talons, with the writing: "The Second Fleet – Norfolk". Dimitri let out a whistle, admiring the document.

"I thought sailors weren't allowed to whistle", said Yevgeni.

"Yes, but only at sea", Dimitri said.

Dimitri continued to look at the pages. He looked mesmerized.

"What is Norfolk?" asked General Okhramenko.

"It's the largest naval base in the world and it's in Virginia, the United States, on the Atlantic coast", Dimitri replied and continued his thorough examination of the papers. "The truth is, I took a look at the pages earlier during our meeting, but I focused on the map and missed the description on the other side. I swear, our guys in Washington are really good. Correction; they are the best."

"So this is what we have here", continued Dimitri in an admiring tone. "This is the navigation training program of the American nuclear assault submarine fleet in the Atlantic Ocean for the month of November 1981. Stunning. Simply stunning."

"I see a map on this page, and the second page has tables", Yevgeni said. "Can you tell us briefly what this data means?"

"The map shows the navigation route from their base on the East Coast of the North American continent, more or less towards the north of Norway, and then they turn south", Dimitri said, tapping on the map with his finger.

"These triangles along the route are reporting points. The submarine must report home when it arrives at any such point along the route. Of course, we will catch it between two reporting points, and I think that will be here."

Dimitri tapped his finger on a certain point on the map.

"Exactly here, northwest of Norway, approximately two hundred nautical miles south of this not very small island called Svalbard. From this place they turn south on their navigation route and sail away."

"And what are these tables?" Yevgeni asked again.

"This is their duty roster, their work schedule. It says which submarine goes out to sea for navigation and when, and their times of arrival at the reporting points. This is simply perfect. I think we have just received the most important brick in the wall that we are about to build."

Yevgeni motioned for his colleagues to leave the derelict hangar. I think I have good reason to contact the Minister of Defense and to report to him on the great headway that we have made, Yevgeni thought. This is the first time that the conversation between us is on my own initiative, but maybe it will be better to wait until the end of the test tomorrow. Who can guarantee that the results will meet expectations? Yevgeni continued to walk besides his teammates as these thoughts raced in his mind.

In a hangar at the ordnance section, Nazarbayev received them with his broad smile. But the Colonel's face showed signs of fatigue; he hadn't had any sleep for two days and nights.

"My friend the Colonel", Yevgeni said to him. "I need you strong and alert tomorrow morning. Have you finished your work here?"

"Yes, I can say that we have finally completed the work. Here, the bomb is ready, and in one or one-and-a- half hours it will be loaded on to the boat. Don't ask me what we went through tonight. We dismantled the bomb, but we couldn't empty it of the explosive, as it was really corroded inside. If I'd used your idea and welded the cone to its top, half of the base would have been demolished in an explosion."

"But I see that the steel cone is installed on the top of the bomb", Yevgeni said quizzically.

"Yes, you see it is connected, not welded. We used special adhesives for metal that I hadn't known existed. They are as strong as welds", Colonel Nazarbayev explained.

Yevgeni approached the Colonel and gave him a brief hug.

"Well done. Come with us. We are going to see the trawler and then you can go and catch a few hours' sleep. We are finished here", said Yevgeni.

Lieutenant Alexey led the team, which was now joined by Colonel Nazarbayev, to an out-of-the-way pier almost hidden from view, where the trawler was moored. The boat was painted black, with a diagonal white stripe adorning its prow. On its stern, its name was printed in Cyrillic letters, and in Latin letters underneath; its name was "Zlatoya Klatzo", meaning "Golden Ring".

Dimitri approached Yevgeni.

"Listen, I'm pleasantly surprised. This is quite a new boat and it looks in very good condition. I also see that it has a modern radar. The Minister's letter has worked wonders. By the way, isn't more fitting to name it Fire Ring rather than

Golden Ring?"

Commander Vitaly Dobrinin, whom Marshal Budarenko's team had met just a short time ago, greeted them on the trawler's gangplank like old friends. General Okhramenko took the lead and led them to the communications room, where a few technicians were still working. The General ordered them to leave the room and shut the door behind them. The team members saw four metal cabinets, each the size of an average washing machine.

"Now", the general said, "they are finalizing their link to the antennas that they installed at dawn, and we will be ready for tomorrow."

Yevgeni motioned Dimitri to come closer to him and the General.

"Tell me, Dimitri", Yevgeni said, "When a submarine arrives at the reporting point, to those triangles on the map, you said that they report to their home base on the East Coast of the United States. Is that correct?"

"Yes, exactly."

"General Okhramenko", Yevgeni said quite severely, "we have not finished our work. Please get a receiver or a listening device from the intelligence section here for those strangely low frequencies that Dimitri mentioned. I can't be sure that the American submarine will navigate exactly according to the schedule printed in the tables here. Perhaps the data is erroneous, and perhaps it is fabricated, and in any case, it can be changed at any time when the submarine is at sea. We must hear for ourselves, with our own ears, the real-time reports from the submarine. Isn't it obvious that this instrument is not sufficient for our needs?"

The General, who was clearly not comfortable being managed by a Colonel, especially one who looked like a university professor, was quite impatient.

"I don't understand you, Colonel; what is not enough for you?"

"Who will operate this instrument? Your communication people or your electronic warfare people?" Yevgeni countered with his own questions. "There must be an intelligence officer here who knows how to listen to naval messages in English. Our friends from Naval Intelligence know exactly who should sit here. It is important that this person is in position during the test tomorrow, even though it is not an integral part of the test."

Yevgeni and Dimitri left the radio room, followed by the General. Yevgeni seemed preoccupied. He looked at Dimitri.

"Tell me, do you think that everything is ready for tomorrow and we aren't forgetting something? It's going too smoothly. I am not supposed to be calm in such situations, and it worries me."

Dimitri was quite confident. "It is only because you are an incurable pessimist", he said.

"You know what the definition of a pessimist is", Yevgeni answered. "A pessimist is an optimist with experience. By the way, do you think we should initiate a call to the Marshal today and keep him updated about our progress?"

"I see that you miss our daily meetings with him. No, don't call him, for two reasons. The first is that tomorrow we will be much wiser, and the second is that our friend, the sixth man, is probably reporting to Moscow every few hours. Forget it. Don't call him today."

"Yes, you're right", concluded Yevgeni. "Let's wait for tomorrow."

CHAPTER 9

An hour had passed since Brigadier General Dimitri and Colonel Yevgeni had boarded K-219, the Navaga class nuclear submarine. In the ship's belly, they were standing beside Captain Yashin, who was sitting in the captain's chair, raised on a metal platform, and looking into the periscope. The submarine had made its way out of the port, slowly sailing from its pier, still above water.

Unlike the chilly atmosphere of their first meeting at Rear Admiral Leonov's headquarters, the submarine Captain now displayed camaraderie, and even friendship, towards his guests. While leaving the port, the Captain had even invited the two officers to spend some time with him on the submarine's upper deck. From the height of the deck, five stories above the water, they looked on with amazement and awe as the submarine's huge hull cut through the water with great power and grace.

Now, the preparations for the dive were frenzied. The sound of a whistle, intermittent and hoarse, filled the dense air of the submarine's belly with urgency. The duty seaman, who sat at his position closest to the commander's post, wearing headphones, read various numbers loudly and quickly; data received and summarized from the submarine's various sections. Loudspeakers were installed the length and width of the ship, and the call Dive-Dive-Dive was broadcast throughout. The submarine commander leaned over the periscope eyepiece, carefully examining the sea into which his awesome war machine was about to sink.

"Five meters, ten meters, seventeen meters", the duty seaman called out the depths into which the submarine was diving.

"I don't like this, Dimitri", whispered Yevgeni.

"You've probably seen too many movies with bursting pipes and flooding inside old submarines. I can promise you that this won't happen to us. Even statistically, the probability of exposure to nuclear radiation here is much higher than the risk of sinking."

"Good, thanks. You've really calmed me down. Do you also know what the probability is for these two things to happen exactly simultaneously, exactly today and exactly in this submarine?"

"No, I don't know, but if we are playing statistics this morning, then the probability of our Minister of Defense having our heads today is so much higher than the probability of something happening to us and to this submarine", Dimitri concluded.

Yevgeni, still terrified, decided not to continue the conversation so as not to give his mate Dimitri the chance to play on his weaknesses.

"One hundred meters, one hundred and ten meters", the duty seaman continued counting out the diving data.

Dimitri looked again at Yevgeni, who had been silent from a depth of thirty-five meters.

"Are you all right?"

"More or less, considering the circumstances. You know

that all is relative, and here is a story. A fellow who wants to commit suicide, throws himself from the twentieth floor. On his way down, on the tenth floor, a neighbor sees him and asks, "How are you doing?" The fellow committing suicide answers: "So far, so good".

Dimitri gave a short bark of laughter, then spoke to Yevgeni quietly.

"I am intentionally not taking you around the submarine to show you the instruments that will measure the blast's data. I don't want any one of the operators to understand that later on, they might encounter such an event. As far as they're concerned, we are totally transparent, no more than tourists."

"You're absolutely right. Everything should be done in the most natural and routine way, as if we were not here at all."

Dimitri looked at his watch. "Very soon we'll be arriving at the point that we set for the submarine, and five minutes after that, the explosion will take place, exactly at 1005 hours."

The Captain summoned them to him with a motion of his hand.

"We will be arriving at the location point that you gave us within two minutes, and there we'll stop. Actually, we're already stopping. You can see here right in front of you, on the diving meter, that we are already at the depth that you requested, two hundred and ninety meters."

"Thank you, Captain", Yevgeni replied, and turned to his mate Dimitri, who seemed restless and preoccupied.

"What's happening, Dimitri? You seem worried. Have you become me?"

Dimitri did not seem to hear Yevgeni's words. He looked at his watch again, then suddenly leapt at Captain Yashin, cluthcing his arm.

"Quickly, quickly, captain! Change direction to three hundred sixty at full steam and maintain a speed of twenty-one knots. Now!"

The submarine commander and Yevgeni had no idea of what had come upon Dimitri at that moment. The captain looked quizzically at Dimitri before responding.

"Are you sure?"

"Yes, yes. This is critical. "Go, go now", Dimitri called out, his voice high-pitched and urgent.

Colonel Yashin took the microphone and the loudspeakers throughout the ship broadcast his order in his quiet and authoritative voice: "Full steam, direction three hundred sixty."

Dimitri looked at Yevgeni with relief. It seemed that a huge load had just been lifted from his shoulders.

"We are three minutes from our test", he said.

"Then explain to me in half a minute, why the sudden outburst?"

"I'll tell you exactly why. I suddenly realized that if the submarine were motionless, our test would not take place under real-life conditions. When the submarine is in motion, there are many environmental noises. For example, the propellers' noise, or the friction between the submarine's girth and the water. Then, if we did the same with the American submarine, it would be in motion. Therefore, I want us to test in real conditions, with noise and vibrations, not under controlled laboratory conditions, while we are standing still and everything around us is quiet."

Dimitri looked at his watch again.

"We have one more minute, and I don't have any idea what to expect."

Yevgeni felt that all their frantic efforts of the last few

days were being channeled into one critical moment. The thoughts raced through his mind. We either continue from here proudly, with heads held high, or someone will have our heads cut off.

"Sir", the duty seaman called out to Captain Yashin, "Position Four is reporting an earthquake detected at one seventy-five degrees. The magnitude is very low and he is trying to confirm the data with several other sources."

"Received", Captain Yashin said, and looked for any reaction from Dimitri and Yevgeni.

Dimitri shrugged his shoulders as if not understanding the meaning of the report. Dimitri turned his back to the seaman beside him and pressed his finger to his lips, warning motioned to the Captain not to say a word.

The seaman called out again.

"Sir, Captain. Position Two detected a distant sound from the same direction."

Dimitri watched Yevgeni's face, which bore a troubled expression.

"I was afraid of this. We have obviously failed", Yevgeni said finally. Dimitri continued watching him without saying a word. Indeed, Yevgeni appeared as if the sky was crashing down on him, and Dimitri tried to think of a way, some way, to lift his mate's spirits.

"Look, Yevgeni. The blast provided the right indications of an earthquake or a nuclear explosion far away. Where we failed is in estimating the correct distance from the blast point, because some acoustic noise from the explosion was sensed in the submarine. What we need to do now is get farther away from the American submarine with the blast, and we need to know by how much. If we get too far, they will still not hear the noise of the explosion, but the earthquake effects on the Richter scale would be either too low or borderline."

The duty seaman called out again.

"Sir, Captain, Number Four crossed data and determined that the epicenter of the quake is within the area of our firing range. That can explain the noise received at position Number Two. Maybe they dropped a big depth charge there."

The submarine commander looked at Dimitri without speaking.

"We have finished", said Dimitri. "We can head back home."

"This submarine has never had such a short mission", Captain Yashin said laconically. He had probably noticed his guests' low spirits, and was taking advantage of this in his own way, adding insult to injury.

"Where do we go from here?" Dimitri asked Yevgeni.

"Most probably, we are already on our way to a gulag in Siberia." Dimitri wrapped his arm round Yevgeni's shoulder.

"Everything will be all right, Mr. Pessimist. We'll come up with a solution. I think you're exaggerating; this is not a total failure, because we did achieve the right effect. The problem is with the acoustic noise. This is not simple, as it depends on the water temperature at the selected site and, of course, also on the sensitivity of the instruments on board the American submarine. I don't think anyone can tell us for certain if their acoustic instruments are more sensitive than those in our own submarines."

"Do you really not know? If not, you should know that they are ahead of us in almost every technological development. I think the last time we were ahead of them in anything was about 20 years ago, April 1961, with Yuri Alexeyevich Gagarin."

Brigadier General Dimitri now decided to leave Yevgeni alone to his self-recrimination. He turned to the submarine commander, and the two naval officers started a navy-related conversation, while Yevgeni remained sitting in his position with his thoughts and calculations.

THE FIVE TEAM MEMBERS SAT IN THE BRIEFING ROOM AT THE Intelligence Section. It was their first meeting following the sea test, from which they had returned just a few minutes before. Most of them did not yet know the test results. Colonel Yevgeni decided to open the discussion by addressing the Kazakh colonel.

"Let's start with you, Colonel Nazarbayev. How did the test go from your point of view?"

"There were no unexpected incidents. Once the bomb was released from the crane, it sank very quickly, and most importantly, the improvised fuse mechanism and its protective shield worked perfectly."

"Excellent", said Yevgeni, and shifted his gaze to General Okhramenko. The General did not wait for Yevgeni to call on him.

"On my part, everybody was actually passive. We only checked that the systems are working. We manned the new position for listening to submarine communications and the operator managed to receive some distant communication traffic from American submarines. That is all, really."

Yevgeni pulled a pack of cigarettes out of his coat pocket and lit one. He exhaled some smoke from the corner of his mouth and turned to Brigadier General Dimitri.

"Please report to our comrades the events that we witnessed in the submarine."

Dimitri described the test results to his teammates. He was very careful not to call the outcome a failure, but rather a situation in which several unknowns of an equation would be problematic to solve. Dimitri shared the dilemma with his teammates - that he was not at all sure that detonating the charge on the seabed was the right way to go, saying that the outcome could be better if the explosion happened on the water's surface. In conclusion, Dimitri said that he thought that the plan was viable, and estimated the likelihood of success at about fifty percent.

When Dimitri finished his account, the team members noticed that Colonel Yevgeni, unlike his recently acquired authoritarian fashion, was not inclined to speak further, and this resulted in informal chats among the team members.

"Colonel Yevgeni!" Colonel Nazarbayev suddenly called out in a loud voice, and the other three team members fell silent.

"Yes, Comrade", Yevgeni replied.

"I've just had a totally insane idea. Why not go for the real thing?" "And what is the real thing?"

"Instead of simulating a nuclear blast and communication blocks etc. etc., why not detonate an actual nuclear artillery shell that fit our requirements exactly", explained Colonel Nazarbayev.

The room turned eerily silent in an instant. Dimitri, the experienced naval officer and intelligence analyst, combed his cropped hair with his fingers, considering this bizarre idea without dismissing it out of hand, and formulating a careful answer. He turned to Colonel Nazarbayev.

"My dear colleague, I think you have defined your idea yourself. It really is insane!"

General Okhramenko cleared his throat, and Dimitri looked at him with respect.

"My friend, Nazarbayev, I think your idea is insane but also extraordinarily clever. At first glance, I find it lacking in one component, and that is that we cannot carry out any preliminary experiment. The experiment is the idea, executed in real time on the day of the operation. Of course, we can't do this without getting prior approval from the Minister of Defense, Marshal Budarenko, but I can take care of that."

Yevgeni drew on the cigarette again and turned to Colonel Nazarbayev.

"Please give us some background. What is this nuclear shell?"

"Our Armed Forces have nuclear artillery shells. They are tactical weapons that were developed to destroy headquarters and troop concentrations the size of brigades and armored divisions. A 152- millimeter shell of this kind, that can be fired from a self-propelled gun, has the power of zero point one megaton, which is equivalent to one hundred thousand tons of TNT. It's the smallest tactical nuclear shell available in our Armed Forces."

Yevgeni interrupted him.

"This little shell is pretty big. To the best of my knowledge, it is about six times more powerful than the bomb dropped on Hiroshima. Is that right?"

"It is true, Colonel, but we would fire the shell into an empty area in the ocean. I estimate the kill radius is in the range of a few kilometers. Four-five kilometers, maybe a little more. In the worst case, some fishermen will die."

"And how are we going to fire this shell?"

"Firing is done from a standard 152 mm self-propelled

gun. In my opinion, although it is very preliminary, we have two options. One, to install the gun on the bow of the boat. This may cause difficulties in operating the gun, especially because of sea motion, waves et cetera. The other option may necessitate reinforcing the area where the gun is deployed. We simply take the Akatsiya, as it is, and place it on the deck with a large pier crane, right in position on the deck."

"Pardon my ignorance, but what is this Akatsiya thing?"

"It's a standard Red Army Artillery Corps self-propelled gun, and we have several thousands of them. If we resolve the issue of weight and loads, the gun will be ready to fire ten minutes after the crane places it on the deck."

"And how much does this Akatsiya weigh?" Yevgeni asked

"Twenty-six tons."

Yevgeni again paused to think, before turning back to Dimitri.

"Brigadier General Dimitri, why are you so quiet? It's important that I get your opinion on this dramatic twist of the plot."

Dimitri sat up in his seat and shot another question at Colonel Nazarbayev.

"Some details are lacking for me to form an opinion. For example, what is the range of this gun?" "Twenty-four kilometers."

"That means that we should let the submarine pass underneath us to the east and wait until it is several tens of kilometers away and only then shoot the shell. I have another question to ask you. Does this shell have a fuse that can detonate at a certain altitude above the surface, or in our case, above water?"

"Yes of course. It is called a shell with a barometric fuse."

Colonel Nazarbayev now seemed encouraged, even enthusiastic, to carry out the idea that he had come up with only a few minutes before.

"If you give me the green light, I can get such a gun and its crew of four within several hours. As for the shell, that would require a personal order from the Minister of Defense, Marshal Budarenko, but that would be your baby, Colonel Yevgeni."

Dimitri expected Yevgeni to reply to the Kazakh Colonel, but Yevgeni turned to him instead.

"Dimitri, you haven't given us your opinion of the new plan. So, please, tell us what you think. I'm anxious to hear it."

"As I see it, we can all agree on this insane, bizarre plan. We should distribute the tasks between us, as I think that within twenty-four hours, we'll have to go for the real thing.

"Yevgeni, you contact the Minister of Defense. I think that your winning argument with him is that with this nuclear shell, we can be ready and on our way as early as tomorrow. Of course, he should issue the order immediately, for the nuclear command to provide us with this shell. Colonel Nazarbayev, you activate your people to deliver the Akatsiya here without delay. We need to take a structural engineer to the trawler. I want him to check the boat's blueprints and tell us exactly where to place these twenty-six tons. Ask Commander Vitaly, the boat's captain, to procure a large tarpaulin to conceal the gun, but not a military one. If they don't have one in stock, they should buy a colorful one in town."

Dimitri leaned towards Yevgeni and they exchanged a few whispers before he continued.

"I suggest that we adjourn now for half an hour, no more. Colonel Yevgeni will try to catch the Minister of Defense;

Colonel Nazarbayev will assign tasks to his team, and when we return, we will study the Americans' training program and come out of here with the final detailed schedule for executing the mission. We'll reconvene here in half an hour. Let's go."

THE TEAM MEMBERS HURRIED TO TAKE THEIR SEATS AROUND THE table where Colonel Yevgeni was already seated. Brigadier Dimitri sat in a corner of the room with a young officer in a naval uniform. A large map was spread over the table and Dimitri held a slide rule and was taking notes in his notebook.

"He'll join us presently", Yevgeni told the team. "We have approval and confirmation from Marshal Budarenko. Two shells will be delivered to us by dawn tomorrow."

Yevgeni turned to Colonel Nazarbayev.

"What have you managed to arrange for us, Colonel?"

"The Akatsiya will be sent to us from an artillery battalion not far from here. They estimate that it will take three or four hours from now, and they are also sending a crew with the gun. The structural engineer is conducting a preliminary investigation at this very minute. He reckons that it won't be a problem to lower the gun onto the amidships deck and not onto the bow; this is preferable not just regarding loads, but also better for the ship's balance. There will also be less sea motion."

Dimitri seemed deep in thought, habitually scratching his head.

"Please tell me", Yevgeni said, turning to him. "Is the bow area of the boat completely clear of antennas or other protruding elements that may be in the shell's trajectory? If the gun is located amidships, will there be any problem?"

"We've checked the issue. The command bridge with the

radar, which is the tallest element on the boat, is at the stern. Therefore, when the gun is located in the middle of the boat, there should be no impediment, especially since the firing will be at an elevation of forty-five degrees. In short, we've checked the issue and there is no obstacle."

In the corner of the room, Dimitri thanked the junior officer for his assistance, dismissed him and then hurried to join his teammates. Yevgeni waited until Dimitri took his seat at the table, and only then continued.

"General Okhramenko, I want to say a few words to you. The role of the radio operator from Intelligence is critical. Only he can change the time of firing, based on the reports that he retrieves from the submarine along its reporting points. It is important to understand that the purpose of all the communication-blocking equipment has not been canceled. The nuclear blast will indeed cause a communication block, but no one can say for certain how long it will last and at what radius from the epicenter of the blast it will be. Therefore, your people should be responsible for all the communication blocks from the time of the firing. From my point of view, it will be compounded security. There is another critical subject, and that is: who will take overall command of the activities, especially of coordinating the timing for firing on the ship? This cannot be done remotely, but from the boat itself, which is under the command of Commander Vitaly, who in effect is nothing but our driver."

Colonel Nazarbayev raised his hand.

"There's no such question here at all, Colonel Yevgeni. This is my responsibility and I have to be aboard the trawler. Everything starts and ends with the firing of this shell, and that is now my baby. I request that you not even think of stationing anyone else aboard that boat."

Yevgeni glanced quickly at Dimitri, whose face was expressionless, yet Yevgeni could see that he was giving him a slight vertical nod of his head as a sign of consent.

"Colonel Nazarbayev, I respect your wish. I could not ask for anyone more responsible and more reliable than yourself for such a supreme and critical mission,."

Colonel Nazarbayev nodded his head in gratitude and smiled with satisfaction. Now, everyone at the table waited for Brigadier General Dimitri to speak. He stood by the table with the paper map rolled in his hand.

"Are you ready?" Yevgeni asked.

Dimitri spread the map out on the table. It was a nautical chart of the Atlantic Ocean with blue and red lines stretched its length and width. A photograph of a submarine was placed on it. Dimitri took the picture and held it up for everyone to see, and began speaking animatedly.

"Comrades, this is our engagement. Please meet the bride, USS 726, the Ohio. She is the creation of an aviation giant, the General Dynamics Corporation. Here is some general data on this vessel. It is a new submarine, having only been in service for two and a half years, since April 1979. It is one hundred and seventeen meters long and thirteen meters wide. Its crew is made up of fifteen officers and one hundred and forty seamen. The submarine is equipped with twenty-four Trident missiles, and its home port is Bangor in the state of Washington."

Yevgeni interrupted.

"Up till now, you're presenting this submarine as if we want to buy her. Dimitri, we're short of time. Please get to the point, to the operational details."

Dimitri smiled. It seemed that he was not about to take Yevgeni's advice.

"Now, having met the bride-to-be, I will tell you when we are set to meet. USS 726 Ohio set sail for navigation exercises nine days ago from Norfolk. Within three days, it will arrive at our rendezvous point here, northwest of Norway, about four hundred kilometers southeast of the island of Svalbard. Here, right here. This is exactly the place."

Dimitri pointed to a red circle on the map, and everybody looked at it.

"If the weather doesn't change drastically, the trawler will require forty hours to reach the rendezvous point, and it must be there on location five to six hours before the American submarine is due. If you work it out for yourselves, you'll see that the trawler must sail tomorrow at noon at the latest."

Brigadier General Dimitri motioned to Colonel Nazarbayev, who came up to him, and the two exchanged whispers in a huddle.

"Do you see this reporting point? The submarine should arrive here in three days' time, at 1012 hours in the morning. You should be at this point exactly. You will wait here another twenty-nine minutes for the submarine to sail away from you eastward, for about eighteen kilometers, and then you will fire your nuclear shell to the west, at exactly 1041 hours. Your firing to the west, and the submarine's movement to the east, will create a distance of forty-two kilometers between the blast epicenter and the submarine. This timetable is sacrosanct. Only you, Colonel Nazarbayev, as the commander in the field, may change it, and only on one condition: only if the Intelligence radio operator, who will be aboard the boat with you, hears with his own ears that the submarine reports from the location points at times that are different to the times on the navigation chart. This is very rare, and it is reasonable to assume that it will not happen this time. Colonel Nazarbayev, you don't have to memorize anything – I've written down everything for you on the chart on this table."

Colonel Yevgeni waited patiently until Dimitri and the Kazakh Colonel looked up from the chart.

"I am asking every one of you again. We have exactly eighteen hours. Each of you should go over his tasks and notes, nudge anyone who needs nudging, and cover all possible corners. We'll meet later next to the trawler. Good luck to everyone and especially to you, my friend Nazarbayev."

The team members began leaving the conference room. Then Colonel Nazarbayev noticed that Yevgeni and Dimitri were still in the room, and he joined them.

"Aren't you coming to the trawler?"

"We need to finish up a few things. We'll join you in a few minutes."

Nazarbayev left the room.

Brigadier General Dimitri looked at Yevgeni, who was sitting at the table, both hands covering his head. He touched him gently on the shoulder.

"My good friend Yevgeni, I know exactly what you're thinking. We have no choice. If it helps ease your conscience, please remember that fifty percent of the decision is down to me. It was a joint decision by the two of us."

"Thank you for your support, Dimitri, but it's almost unbearable, even with this fifty percent. He is a good man, the Kazakh officer. He is simply a very good man."

CHAPTER 10

Svetlana, faithful private secretary to Vladimir Petrovich Yermolov, General Secretary of the Communist Party, the Head of State of the Soviet Union and the Commander in Chief of its Armed Forces, glanced at the large wall clock across from her desk. She got up and hurried to the General Secretary's office.

"Gospodin Vladimir Petrovich Yermolov. I wish to remind you that the Minister of Defense, Marshal Budarenko, will arrive in five minutes' time to see you."

"Yes, I remember", the Secretary replied, without lifting his eyes from the document he was reading.

Svetlana welcomed her uncle, Marshal Budarenko, with a broad smile. Her sharp senses detected right away that the Minister was in good spirits and in a much better mood than usual this morning. She led him to the General Secretary's office, but before he went in, he pulled her into a hug and kissed her on the cheek. She let out a giggle. This is interesting, she thought. What's causing this grumpy uncle of mine to feel so happy this early in the morning? Maybe today, for a change, there is a better chance than usual that his conversation with Gospodin Yermolov will be peaceful and produce a better outcome.

The Minister of Defense took his seat at the heavy oak desk across from his superior, and only then did the General Secretary finish reading the document and place it on the desk.

"Good morning to you, Mister Secretary."

"Good morning, Minister. Am I correct in saying that your mood is better than usual this morning? Is there a particular reason for it? Please tell me, as it may also lift my own spirits."

The General Secretary said this without expression. The Minister of

Defense smiled and made himself comfortable in the chair.

"It is a simply glorious day. The whole of Moscow is white and the sun is shining. But I am here to brief you on the progress of our deployment on the border of the German Democratic Republic."

One of the female office workers entered the room, bowed her head slightly, and placed a silver tray with a teakettle and two glasses on the table. The two watched in silence until she left the room.

"I am listening, Marshal. Speak up."

"For three days now we've been mobilizing our forces to the border areas of the German Democratic Republic. This is a huge logistical operation, and far from simple. We've been using trains, and I've commandeered almost every railroad engine and car from all corners of the country. What is delaying us a little is the fact that our trains travel across Poland only at nighttime. There are two reasons for this. One is that they don't have too many railway systems and I don't want to shut down their regular service lines during the day; not least because it would signal to the West that this is an especially urgent action. The second reason is that, of course, during the night, the Americans and their friends in NATO won't be able to estimate the size of our forces, particularly as these are typical winter nights."

"And how is the collaboration with the Poles? Do you want me to talk to someone who can expedite things?"

"No, Mister General Secretary. There is no need. They are collaborating exceptionally well. At night, no Polack train moves. They have cleared everything to make it one hundred percent available to us only."

The General Secretary drank his tea and examined the face of his Minister of Defense.

"How long will this continue?"

"This is a tremendous logistical operation. It's not only tanks; it also includes fuel, ordnance, supplies, logistical head-quarters, full operational headquarters of brigades, divisions and armies. In short, vast masses. We shall complete most of the deployment within two or three days. But we'll still need the trains to continue conveying supplies and equipment on an ongoing basis indefinitely."

The General Secretary seemed ill at ease. He contracted his eyebrows and scratched his chin.

"I think we should get this done as soon as possible. I don't think we can trust the Poles for long, especially after we enter Germany. After all, we're not going there to entertain residents and parade our forces, right? When blood starts flowing, and there is no doubt that blood will be shed, Poland itself may start an insurgency in solidarity with their German brethren."

"I don't really think so", the Minister of Defense replied. "Who will try raising his head in Poland when the Red Army has such a presence in its territory? That would be unthinkable."

General Secretary Yermolov shifted his weight uneasily, seemingly not convinced by his Minister's answer.

"In order for it to stay unthinkable, as you say, the operation in Germany must be swift, and with a minimum of casualties. If you can accomplish this, then the Americans and NATO will need less time to calm down."

"Mister Secretary, regarding the Americans and NATO, I propose that you send the American President a conciliatory letter, explaining that this is business that we have with our sister states and that we have no aggressive intentions towards them. What do you think?"

The General Secretary took another sip from his cup of tea. He raised his eyebrows, and a hint of an ironic smile played at the corners of his mouth.

"I don't believe what I'm hearing. Marshal Budarenko; is this you? What happened? Has the tiger turned into a sheep?"

The Minister of Defense opted not to answer the General Secretary, and continued staring at him.

"By the way, dear Marshal, I think your idea of the letter to Washington is excellent, and that is exactly what I will be doing before the end of the day."

THE UNITED STATES ARMY EUROPEAN COMMAND HEAD-QUARTERS was located in a large military base near the city of Frankfurt. The large conference room in the Operations Section was filled with the senior commanding officers of the United States forces stationed on European soil. Those with higher ranks took their seats in the first row of chairs, which was already filled, except for one empty chair at its center. The headrest on the chair bore the name Thomas C. Bell, and four stars were printed on it in gold. Along the row, the United

States Army's most senior officers were seated beside top U.S. Navy Admirals. George N. Kelly, Commander of the U.S. Air Forces European Air Command, based in Ramstein, also sat there in his blue uniform, with his pilot's wings hardly visible above the rows of ribbons, somewhat aloof towards his green-and-white uniformed colleagues.

In the second row, an officer in different-looking formal attire was seated. He was NATO's Liaison Officer to the United States Armed Forces, wearing a French General's cap that looked like a gilded upside- down cooking pot, setting the French General aside from the others. He wore a red silk scarf around his neck, tucked neatly under his shirt collar. A few seats to his right, a German officer sat in his unassuming gray military suit.

"Attention!" was heard, and all those in attendance rose to their feet. General Thomas Bell, wearing camouflage fatigues, strode into the room. Many stories and legends had been told of the colorful military career of this son of Texas. He was not a tall man, but had an athletic, muscular build. As an ex-Marine, his short-cropped hair was no more than stubble, a few days old. He was known as an outspoken, maverick officer, who had been rebuked numerous times for his undiplomatic, often provocative, language, especially towards the Soviet Union. Behind his back, some people dubbed him Little Patton.

Thomas Bell walked directly to the stage and stood behind a wooden podium adorned with the seal of the United States Armed Forces. The large expanse of wall behind him was covered with large maps of Central and Eastern Europe, overlaid with transparent plastic sheets that bore many tactical markings in red, blue, and black.

General Bell wished his audience a good morning and

instructed them to be seated. Holding a long stick, the General addressed them.

"The Red enemy has apparently decided to test our nerves, and I'm not sure that it really wants to test us. The enemy has been pushing vast amounts of armor westward for the past three days. In the next few hours, the Supreme Command will up the alert for all the United States Armed Forces, wherever they are, to DEFCON 3. It will require each of you to ensure that all your units, on land and at sea and in the air, open their operations files, examine and revise their details and memorize all battle orders. At this stage – and I emphasize: at this stage – training will continue as usual. We will now hear an intelligence update."

General Bell walked to his seat in the first row, and his place at the podium was taken by a representative of Military Intelligence, a Colonel wearing light khaki camouflage fatigues.

"Good morning, everyone."

A few officers murmured a greeting.

"For three nights now the Red Army has been transferring, mainly by rail, very large forces, mostly armored forces, into Western Poland, close to the border with Eastern Germany. So far, in our estimation, about eight thousand tanks and some two thousand armored personnel carriers have been transported, and the flow of vehicles and materials is continuing."

Whispers were heard throughout the room. The Colonel paused for several seconds until silence was restored in the hall.

"I wish to make it clear, so that you understand, that such a scope of troop deployment has never been seen before. This is the size of more than forty armored divisions! Just for a sense of scale, in 1968, when the Soviet Union invaded and occupied

Czechoslovakia, they only deployed about two thousand tanks. According to radio communications that we've intercepted, more tanks will continue to be moved westwards tonight. The scope of activity is so vast that no Polish civilian trains run at night. One can say that all railroads have been seized for the Russian military trains.

"On the diplomatic front, our President received tonight an urgent letter from the General Secretary of the Communist Party in the Soviet Union. In this letter, Secretary Yermolov explains that this is an internal problem of the Warsaw Pact. The letter is quite uncharacteristic, as it lacks the traditional threats of 'do not interfere and if you do interfere, be prepared to suffer the consequences' etc. etc. I must confess that our experts are quite confounded by this letter. Some of them claim that the conciliatory and nonthreatening language is meant to lull us into a false sense of security regarding an operation that could exceed the limits of repressing the insurrection in the German Democratic Republic."

General Bell interrupted the Colonel.

"I agree with that", he called out from his seat for everyone to hear. "It makes a lot of sense. They don't need so many forces just to suppress civil disobedience in Eastern Germany."

A young officer entered the room, saluted, and handed the Colonel on the stage a piece of paper seemed to have been torn off a teleprinter roll. The Colonel glanced at the paper and placed it on the podium before him.

"Actually, tonight is extremely critical. If we see that the transfer of forces continues at the same rate tonight, and I don't want to even think about the next nights, then we will face a serious problem with them. There are several elements that we call preparatory threat indicators, which point to later belligerent actions, if the intention is indeed for Soviet forces to cross East Germany and continue westward toward our territory in West Germany.

"These indicators would include the transfer to the front of large engineering corps and many artillery batteries; in addition, deployment of fighter jet and helicopter squadrons west of the front. It goes without saying that they will have to advance anti-aircraft missile batteries. We have enough means at our disposal to detect their movements almost in real time, regardless of the weather. It is important to emphasize that at this moment, we are not there yet. Without the added elements that I mentioned before, they will have the capacity, albeit excessive and exaggerated, to suppress the uprising in Eastern Germany. However, they will not have enough to engage our forces. Of course, this is the complete opposite of their usual tactics, namely, to push forward without the close support of attack aircraft and an anti-aircraft missile umbrella."

The Colonel picked up the message he had received a few minutes before and read it again. He looked at Gerald Bell across from him.

"Precisely on this subject of preparatory threat indicators that must be present before war, our intelligence teams have intercepted an interesting conversation. The conversation was made from the base of an artillery battalion stationed several hundred kilometers southwest of Moscow. All the details of that conversation are here, and the people there are talking about preparations for redeployment, and also about loading onto a train. It may be innocent, but it may also be the first of those indicators which I noted before, now being realized."

The Colonel completed his briefing, and General Bell took his place behind the podium.

"We have heard, with great concern, worrying figures that must trouble every one of us. I'll start with the letter that was sent to our President. This is not typical of the Red enemy as I know it, and I know it at least as well as our intelligence people. In my opinion, this letter has only one purpose: lulling us into complacency. If they continue their unprecedented use of the trains tonight, and haul more tanks into Poland, then by tomorrow the situation as I see it will not have changed, and I will explicitly recommend to Washington, by virtue of my rank, to raise our alertness to DEFCON 2. When this happens, you must halt all training activities throughout your units. All our units will leave their bases for their battle deployment areas and positions and complete their preparations for engaging the enemy."

General Bill waved his finger to the General in charge of the Air Force sitting across from him. The Air Force General sat up in his chair.

"You know that our forces are numerically inferior to the enemy's, in everything to do with tanks and artillery pieces. This is your opportunity to prove to the sages at the Pentagon that they were right to shower you and your friends with so many billions of dollars instead of procuring more tanks and guns for us. You'd better not disappoint me. I expect to raise the alert to number two tomorrow, and then all your aircraft will be there ready on the tarmac, fully loaded for a thirty-minute notice to take off."

General Bell then turned to the Intelligence Colonel.

"I want to say a few more things, especially to you, Colonel, and please forward this to your commanding officers. We all agree that the forces that the enemy has concentrated for entry into Eastern Germany are exaggerated and unreasonable. I'll tell you even more. This force is now exaggerated by any scale, not just for suppressing civil disobedience there, but also for a scenario where the East German Armed Forces resist the invader and fight him on the battlefield. Now I want to ask you a question. I'm sure you know that every unit larger than a battalion in the East German military has Soviet officers attached. The enemy certainly knows and recognizes his own officers, that he himself sent there. Do you really think that the Communist East German military will fight them? Please answer me."

The Colonel in the camouflage fatigues stood up.

"Sir, we have no disputes with you on this point. Your opinion on this point matches our opinion. Our official evaluation says that the East German military will not engage the Red Army in battle."

The General nodded his head in satisfaction before continuing.

"Now, gentlemen, I really don't understand you guys in intelligence. If you agree with me, then it must be clear to you that to suppress civil disobedience, no one needs thousands of tanks, as it makes better sense to base your forces on armored personnel carriers, not tanks. Therefore, only a fool can't see that all these tanks are intended to engage us, or deter us, over here. Don't give me your answer now, but give it to me tomorrow, with an authorized assessment from Intelligence. Not what you personally think, but how the Intelligence Division in its entirety explains this absurdity. In my opinion, tomorrow morning you will also come to agree with my evaluation and understanding. The enemy will use East Germany only as a transit point or a staging point to continue rolling on towards us.

"It doesn't take a great expert to see the reason for this maneuver by the enemy. Their sister countries' regimes are already shaky. They are anxious that the dissent will spill over and spread into the Soviet Union itself. What have others done anywhere in the world, dozens of times, in similar situations? They start a war with their neighbors to rally their people behind their army and regime. This is not a new phenomenon. Has the enemy not heard of it before? I tell you again, those SOBs want a war, and that's what they're going to get!"

"For our meeting tomorrow, I want each of you to bring up-to-date reports of the numbers of viable materials and personnel in all your units. Also, bring inventory stock reports of ordnance and fuel. Hand this report to my deputy and we'll check what we need to request from our hosts here and from Washington. Now let's get to work because there's a lot to be done. We'll meet here tomorrow at the same time."

All the officers rose to their feet when General Thomas Bell left the room at his swift Marine pace, adjusting his camouflage baseball cap on his head.

CHAPTER 11

THE FOUR MEMBERS OF MARSHAL BUDARENKO'S SPECIAL team stood on the gray, dilapidated pier 4 of the Murmansk naval port, wearing thick storm coats and fur caps adorned with the red star and gold laurel leaves of the Soviet Navy. Colonel Yevgeni, Brigadier General Dimitri, General Vitaly Okhramenko and the KGB operator whom the others had dubbed the Sixth Man, watched the small tugboat towing the much bigger trawler out of the port. In the bitterly cold winter air, one could cut the tension with a knife, and each of them kept to himself.

The trawler, with their mate Colonel Nazarbayev aboard, sailed away into the horizon.

Colonel Yevgeni broke the silence.

"Let's go. The plane is waiting for us. There is nothing for us to do here anymore. We can also pray in Moscow."

Yevgeni caught Dimitri's hand and drew him away from the group.

"Did you deliver the envelope to Captain Yashin, the submarine captain?"

"Yes. I did."

"What did you tell him?"

"Exactly what we agreed upon. That only when the trawler

arrives at the location point and stops, is he permitted to open the envelope."

The two continued to walk side by side, each deep in thought. Then Yevgeni spoke in a soft voice.

"Tell me, Dimitri. Is the Kazakh married? Does he have children?"

"No. He's not married and he has no children", Dimitri answered, then added, "Well, with children, sometimes it's difficult to know, but at least as far as he knows, he has no children."

Dimitri paused for a moment, before asking: "Say, Yevgeni, doesn't it seem more logical to you that we run this operation from here, from Murmansk?"

"You may be right on a logical level, with this operation being mainly Naval, but my friend, you are forgetting two things. One is that we hardly have anything to manage anymore; at most we can monitor the events that we have cooked up. Two, the Minister probably prefers our necks close to him, closer to the noose, and he has his own reasons."

"Well, it seems that you are right again. We return to Moscow. And, as usual, thank you for the encouragement."

They quickened their pace and rejoined their three colleagues.

A day and a night had passed, and the trawler was still cutting its way through the North Sea, its bow pointing northwest. Up to a few hours before, the boat crew could discern, on the port side, from a great distance in the cold clear air, the northern snow-covered cliffs of Norway. From time to time, they detected small icebergs in the water, but it did not cause much concern, as this sophisticated vessel could detect any iceberg in its way and had some capacity to function as an icebreaker.

Colonel Nazarbayev sat in the cabin of the ship's captain, Commander Vitaly. The captain, true to his Soviet military discipline, did not try to extract from Colonel Nazarbayev any details, not even hints, of their shared mission. Not once did Nazarbayev wonder about the captain's apparent indifference. If I were the captain, the Colonel thought, and someone had placed a self-propelled gun on my boat's deck, I couldn't contain my curiosity. Indeed, Commander Vitaly is a strange bird, or perhaps he has his own secrets in this operation, unbeknownst to me.

Commander Vitaly noticed that his colleague was deep in thought and decided to start a conversation.

"You are a field rat, after all. How do you feel on my boat?"

"Yes, it's true that in the past few years I have been what you call a field rat, and generally speaking, I much prefer to be on solid ground, but here's something that may surprise you. I was born in a city called Atyrau in Kazakhstan, which is a port city on the coast of the Caspian Sea. My uncle, my mother's brother, earned his living for many years fishing sturgeon, from whose eggs black caviar is produced. That is the best and most expensive of all fish roe. When I was a boy, I would go out to sea with him on weekends and holidays, so I do have quite a few sea hours under my belt."

"Black caviar, you say? Then he made a very good living, your uncle." "Yes, I might say that he supported us financially."

The two continued their small talk, just to pass the time and to ease their boredom on the long journey to their destination.

"Luckily, the weather is with us", said Vitaly. "I think we may even arrive at our destination half an hour early. How are your four gunners doing down there? Have they thrown up their meal yet?"

"I'm glad you reminded me, Commander. I'll go pay them a visit now.

Thank you for the tea, Captain."

The four men in the crew of the self-propelled gun were sitting nearby and chatting, and when they noticed Colonel Nazarbayev approaching, they stood up quickly. They wore green coveralls and blue puffy seamen's coats which made them look like inflatable dolls. The gun was completely covered with a blue tarp.

"How are you, gunners?"

"We are fine, Colonel, except for Gregory. He has already thrown up several times", replied the crew leader.

The colonel looked at Gregory's young face. He was still pale.

"Remind me, soldier. What is your role in the crew?" "I'm the driver, Sir."

"Good then, I have an easy task for you, and after you do it, you can go to one of the ship's crew and ask for pills against seasickness."

"And what is the task, Sir?"

"Lift the blue tarp only on one side, get into the driver's seat, and start the engine. Then let the engine run for five minutes. I don't want us to have a problem with the engine, the battery, or the hydraulics system tomorrow."

The driver turned quickly back to the gun and rolled up the tarp with the help of two of his crew mates. He then opened the heavy steel driver's hatch in front of the gun and disappeared into it, with only the top of his head visible. Two minutes later, the din of the self-propelled gun's engine was heard throughout the ship. Several of the ship's crew gathered near the tank-like vehicle to watch this strange and terrifying behemoth, which had made itself comfortable right in the middle of the deck of their civilian trawler. Thick gray smoke rose above the rear part of the vehicle, disappearing quickly in the cool air. Several minutes later, the driver shut down the engine and emerged from the vehicle, stretching the tarp over the gun again.

"Do you know what type of shell you'll be shooting tomorrow?" Colonel Nazarbayev asked the gun crew.

The older gunner in the crew was eager to reply.

"Yes, Sir, I saw the container of the shell and all its markings. I have never shot a shell like this, but as far as the firing process, there is no difference between this shell and any other."

"Exactly. By the way, I don't think anyone on this planet has ever fired such a shell. Now, the details. Firing will be executed tomorrow at 1041 hours exactly, unless we receive new data which will force us to change the firing time. That is also the reason why we'll arrive at the firing location about five hours earlier. You'll have enough time to get organized, to perform meteorological checks, and to be ready to fire on time. Firing will be to the west, direction 275 degrees, to maximum range. Another important thing: from the moment of firing, you'll remain down here, constantly facing East. If you have questions, now is the time."

The gun crew leader was hesitant. Colonel Nazarbayev encouraged him to speak up.

"Sir, I apologize for raising this issue, but did anyone check to make sure that when we fire the gun, the recoil will not cut through the deck and we won't sink into the sea together with the gun? I don't know exactly how to calculate the recoil, but the force is tremendous, enough to shake the ground when the gun is on land."

"I can remind you how to calculate recoil", replied Colonel Nazarbayev, whose expertise included precisely such calculations. "It is the mass of the shell multiplied by its speed. But you have nothing to fear, Sergeant Major. Our Navy's engineers made all the calculations and everything is in order. You should know that if the gun sinks into the sea, then we all sink with it and with the boat, and personally, I still have plans for the future. Worry not."

Colonel Nazarbayev looked at his watch again, as he had done dozens of times in the past hour. He felt alertness mixed with an almost uncontrollable excitement. The gun crew had already removed the tarp cover, and the Colonel again checked his watch. The hands showed 1002 hours. In ten minutes, he thought, the American submarine will arrive at the reporting point, which is exactly where we have been waiting for the past six hours. We'll wait 29 minutes, which will probably seem like an eternity, and then fire the gun. The thoughts continued to race through his head, and he needed all his powers of self-control to keep calm and focus on his mission.

The sleek, super-modern USS 726 Ohio nuclear submarine had, by now, been submerged for the twelfth consecutive day, maintaining a constant diving depth, speed, and direction. This duration of its stay underwater was not exceptional, as Ohio class submarines could even stay underwater for ninety consecutive days. Navigation at depth was routine and uneventful. Once in a few days, in order to break the monotony of the long journeys, the crew would be called to their battle positions without prior notice, not knowing ahead of time whether it was a drill or a state of war.

The ship's commander was Captain Frank Butcher, who was considered a meteor in the United States Navy. Captain Butcher made regular radio contact with his sister submarine USS 729 Georgia, which was ahead of them by exactly twenty-four hours, on exactly the same navigation course.

The phone in the Captain's position rang, and a red light on the phone was flashing.

"Captain Butcher", he answered.

"Sir, sonar station reporting what looks like a medium-size trawler three and a half miles ahead on our course. The vessel is stationary and we will pass directly underneath it."

"Got it", the Captain confirmed, and placed the telephone handset back in its cradle.

"Sir", this time it was the duty seaman sitting next to the Captain's chair.

Captain Butcher turned to him.

"Speak", he ordered.

"I have just been told by Communications that a top-secret urgent message has arrived from supreme headquarters in Annapolis and they are deciphering it now. They say the message should be ready in two to three minutes."

"Tell them to bring it here as soon as they're done." "Yes, Sir!"

The submarine's Chief Communications Officer appeared soon afterward and handed his commander an envelope. Captain Butcher opened the envelope and read the deciphered telegram, then folded the piece of paper and shoved it in his shirt pocket.

"Dismissed", he told the Communications officer.

The Cptain walked quickly to the wall where the chart with the full navigation course was posted. He examined the map for several seconds before returning to his chair. He then picked up the microphone, and his voice now echoed from the dozens of loudspeakers throughout the submarine.

"This is Captain Butcher speaking. Effective immediately, turn to direction 175. I repeat, immediately turn to direction 175. Rise to depth 150 meters, 150 meters. Full steam, maximum speed. Attention, crew of Ohio 726. The Navy has just raised the state of alert to Grade 2. I repeat, Grade 2. This is only one grade below all-out war. Our navigation drills are discontinued indefinitely from this moment, and we shall now assume our battle positions. Pay attention to anything out of the ordinary."

The submarine's Deputy Commander burst into the Captain's station. "What's going on, Captain?"

"It isn't very clear, but there seems to be some serious problem in Europe, probably with the Reds."

COLONEL NAZARBAYEV WAS NOW IN THE TRAWLER'S RADIO ROOM, next to the Naval Intelligence radio operator. He continued to glance frequently at his watch, and now he turned to the operator for the third time in the past two minutes.

"Are you sure you've heard no report from the submarine? It passed its reporting point 19 minutes ago. You heard nothing? Maybe we have a problem with the receiver or the antenna?"

"Sir, everything is working and everything is in order. I 've been hearing quite a few radio communications, even more than usual. This submarine 726 hasn't reported anything yet."

Colonel Nazarbayev ran out of the communications room

and arrived breathlessly at the self-propelled gun, which was now uncovered, its engine running with a deafening noise. The Colonel stopped near the gun and checked his watch again. Three more minutes, he said under his breath, three more minutes. The gun crew leader gazed at him expectantly, but because of the great noise from the gun's engine, the Colonel could only wave his hand at the gunner from a distance, holding up three fingers. The gunner raised his thumb in confirmation.

The Colonel looked at his watch yet again. His heart was beating with such force that the Colonel felt that it would burst.

CAPTAIN YASHIN, THE K-219 NUCLEAR SUBMARINE COMMANDER, looked through his periscope again. From a great distance, he detected the trawler, which he had been following for almost two days and nights now. He folded the periscope handles and returned to his seat. The Colonel pulled a sealed brown envelope out of his shirt pocket. He tore it open and extracted a note with several typewritten lines. Having read through the message, he put the letter back into his shirt pocket, sank into his chair, and exclaimed in disbelief.

"B'liad!* B'liad!! Bunch of B'liad!!!"[6]

---

6   B'liad: A whore, in Russian

CHAPTER 12

IN MOSCOW, SVETLANA SHOWED THE UNITED STATES AMBAS-SADOR into the office of the General Secretary of the Communist Party of the Soviet Union. Unlike his past visits, this time the Ambassador did not utter a word. He wore a severe expression and was obviously very upset. General Secretary Vladimir Petrovich Yermolov motioned him to sit across from his desk with no greeting. He then looked at his watch and turned to Svetlana.

"It is now ten minutes past ten, and where is the Minister of Defense? I requested his presence at this meeting with the Ambassador. Try to find him again."

"Yes, Mister Secretary." Svetlana replied, and hurried out of the room.

The Secretary continued to read a document that he held in his hand, and spoke to his guest without lifting his eyes from the paper.

"Mister Ambassador, you have exactly ten minutes. Now, please tell me what is so urgent and why you threatened that if we do not meet, there would be 'grave consequences' et cetera."

The Secretary put the document back on his desk and looked straight at the American ambassador. Only then did he notice that the Ambassador was extremely agitated.

"Mister General Secretary, I understand that you have decided to start a war against us and our European allies. I have come to notify you on behalf of the President of the United States that all our forces, including our strategic air and sea forces, are already on high alert, and only if …"

The furious General Secretary interrupted the Ambassador mid- sentence, hitting his desk forcefully with his fist. His face was red with indignation.

"What the hell are you talking about? I don't need your approval to handle an insurrection in the German Democratic Republic!"

The American Ambassador now spoke very undiplomatically, raising his voice.

"Does Mister Secretary need to mobilize over 20,000 tanks, thousands of armored personnel carriers and thousands of guns to pacify a few thousand civilians and demonstrators? Are the dozens of squadrons of jet fighters, surface-to-air missile batteries, and helicopters that have advanced to forward bases in the last twenty-four hours – is all this force also intended to suppress striking workers in the German Democratic Republic? We have intelligence, solid confirmed knowledge, that even this is not the end of your mobilization and that you are intending to push more and more divisions to the front. The Pentagon is convinced that this insane order of battle has only one purpose, and that is the occupation of West Germany, or even Western Europe!"

The General Secretary was too shocked to reply. He couldn't believe his ears and his fury was boundless. He summoned all his might to contain his rage, trying to hide it from the American Ambassador.

Suddenly, and to the Ambassador's astonishment, the General Secretary rose from behind his desk, walked around the table and approached the Ambassador, who scrambled to his feet. The General Secretary placed his hand on the Ambassador's shoulder and spoke very slowly to his face.

"Look me in the eye, Mister Ambassador, and tell your President that you have heard me, with your own ears, stating that we have no intention of attacking you or your allies in Europe. We have no intention of attacking you. Now, did you understand me or should I say it again? We have no intention of attacking you!"

The door suddenly opened. Svetlana stood at the entrance.

"Gospodin Vladimir Petrovich Yermolov, the Minister of Defense

Marshal Budarenko is here. Shall I let him in?"

"Not now", the Secretary shot back in anger. "Let him wait outside."

Several minutes later, as the American Ambassador was leaving the General Secretary's room, he walked past Marshal Budarenko, who bowed his head very slightly in disdain.

The Minister of Defense entered the General Secretary's room. His face was sullen. He leaned forward against the Secretary's desk with his fists resting on it.

"You humiliate me, and what's worse, in the presence of the United States Ambassador? Why did you leave me cooling my heels outside? Why did you do this to me?"

The Secretary sprang like a tiger from his seat and walked towards the Minister of Defense. He pointed to the chair and thundered, "Sit down! From this moment on, only I will speak and you will not say a word."

The Minister quickly sat in the chair. The Secretary was

pacing back and forth behind the back of the Minister, who couldn't make out his superior's behavior. The Secretary continued pacing the room like a lion in its cage.

"What in heaven's name do you think you're doing, Marshal? I give you my approval to enter the German Democratic Republic, and you go behind my back and mobilize enough masses to flood Western Europe? Where do you want to stop? On the coast of the Atlantic Ocean? Have you lost your mind? The Americans, with all their 10,000 nuclear warheads, are already on high alert because of you, only because of you. You leave me no choice. I will have to fire you. Yes, fire you."

General Secretary Yermolov continued pacing behind his Minister of Defense and accusing him. He repeated the information that he had just heard from the American Ambassador to the ears of his Minister of Defense.

COLONEL YEVGENI AND HIS FOUR TEAM MEMBERS HAD JUST ENTERED the underground command headquarters in the secret base outside of Moscow. It was Gregory, the team's coordinator, who summoned them to the war room. The bunker buzzed with activity like a beehive. Many soldiers sat before large communication instruments, strange sounds were heard, and green and red indicator lights were flashing with increasing frequency.

Judging by the awe, perhaps even the fear, displayed by the soldiers in the bunker towards Gregory, the team members realized that this unassuming man held a very senior position on the base in which they had already spent quite a few days.

Gregory and his teammates sat in a side room surrounded by glass walls, known as The Aquarium. The unbearable tension felt by Yevgeni and his teammates made them reticent and solemn, each lost in thought. Every few seconds, they glanced at the clock on the wall and at their wristwatches.

The glass door opened and a soldier burst in to hand Gregory a sheet of paper that the teleprinter had just spat out. Gregory hardly glanced at it before he suddenly shot out of his chair, shouting.

"Now! Now, get me the Minister of Defense. Right now!"

"What happened?" It was Brigadier General Dimitri who wanted to know what had gone wrong, but Gregory ignored him and shouted again.

"I said, at once. Get me Marshal Budarenko now!"

To everyone's astonishment, Dimitri got up and literally pulled the sheet of paper out of Gregory's hands. Gregory remained in his seat, not responding, his eyes on the soldiers walking back and forth outside the aquarium. Dimitri started reading the paper quickly, and Yevgeni came closer, trying to read it as well.

A soldier was heard behind the door.

"Sir, the Minister is with the General Secretary. I am speaking with the

General Secretary's private secretary. She can't disturb them now."

Before the soldier had finished his words, Gregory jumped out of his seat and ran frantically to him, grabbing the telephone from his hand.

"Miss Svetlana. I must speak with the Minister now, this minute. I understand that he is with the General Secretary, but this is an emergency. The Minister will never forgive you if you do not get him to come out now and speak to me. This is a matter of life and death."

"Very well. I will try", Svetlana replied across the line.

Gregory watched the clock in desperation. The clock showed forty minutes past ten. Within one minute, the firing of the nuclear shell would take place. Why the hell wasn't the Minister coming out? He hit the table in frustration. Suddenly, he reached to the soldier sitting next to him, shaking his shoulder violently.

"Get the trawler immediately", he shouted. "Now!"

The Minister of Defense's familiar voice was heard on the other side of the line. The Minister sounded indignant.

"Gregory, you'd better have a good reason for this dumb thing you're doing. Have you gone insane? What the hell happened?" The Minister's voice went up when asking the question.

"Mister Minister, we received a message from our people in Washington that just a few minutes ago, all training activity in the United States Navy was discontinued and all navy servicemen were ordered to man their battle positions."

"So?" the Minister yelled.

"It means, Sir, that at these very seconds, we are firing a shell into nowhere, without a purpose, because their submarine is not there anymore."

There was a chilling silence on the other side of the phone line, which lasted several seconds, after which the Minister barked again.

"Then stop them, you idiot", and the telephone line went dead. The Minister had hung up on his man on the front lines.

"What about the trawler?" Gregory shouted at the soldier near him, while his eyes followed the dials of the large clock on the wall.

"I can't make contact with the trawler, Sir", the soldier replied meekly.

"It's strange. I'm trying and trying and they don't hear me."

"Then try again and again and again and again until they hear you." Gregory's last sentence was uttered in a much more subdued voice, as if he was beginning to realize, deep inside, that he was too late. He crumpled like a deflated balloon. He fell heavily into the nearest chair and looked as pale as a man staring death in the face.

Yevgeni approached Gregory. He held him by the arm.

"It is already too late. Come, let's go back to our conference room and think together about what we can do, looking forward, and what we can recommend to the Minister of Defense. Let's think together how we can explain this nuclear blast in the North Sea. I already have some ideas in the back of my mind. Come; let's go talk about it in our conference room."

Gregory, his spirit broken, rose to his feet without replying, and let Yevgeni lead him to the door without resistance. The rest of the team joined them and made their way out in absolute silence.

SVETLANA ENTERED THE GENERAL SECRETARY'S ROOM. THE SHOUTING session with the Minister of Defense had reached her ears and she understood very well that her boss was especially agitated today.

"Gospodin Vladimir Petrovich Yermolov, the Chairman of the Committee for State Security has arrived, at your request. Does Gospodin wish to be served tea and biscuits?"

"Yes, thank you."

The General Secretary watched Svetlana as she left the room. I'm so lucky to have someone so quiet and efficient, he thought. Here is a person whom I can trust completely.

The Committee Chairman, or in his better known title,

Chief of the KGB, took his seat opposite the General Secretary. He immediately noticed that the Secretary was restless.

"Mister Secretary, has something happened? How can I help you?"

"Yes, a lot has happened, and a lot is still happening. These are my orders. I want you to follow Marshal Budarenko twenty-four hours a day. I want to receive a report every few hours on what he does, who he meets with, what he says, what he eats, when he urinates, and I also want to know the level of sugar in his urine. Everything, I want to know everything. You hear me? Everything! This unscrupulous man is a loose cannon, and he is dragging us into a hot war with the United States. I gave him my approval for X, and he went and did X and Y and Z. This insane bastard has no limits. He will destroy us all. Do you understand? Have I made myself clear?"

"Yes, Mister Secretary. Everything is clear and it will be done immediately."

"Thank you. That's all."

CAPTAIN FRANK BUTCHER SAT IN THE CAPTAIN'S CHAIR OF THE USS 726 Ohio, examining a chart with the submarine's new route. The seaman in charge of briefing him with reports from all the ship's sections sat beside him.

"Now, check when we are supposed to arrive at our battle position", the captain ordered the seaman.

A minute later, the seaman returned to Captain Butcher.

"Sir, the navigation station reports that we will arrive at our battle position in nine hours and twenty-two minutes. But there is a preliminary report that I've just received, of a strong seismic event that caused ground motion. It may be an earthquake."

"OK. Go ahead and collect data."

"Sir", the seaman said again a moment later, "This is very strange. I have just received an unexplained acoustic event from that exact direction. They say it sounds like a continuous, muffled explosion."

"Give me the direction."

"Sir, it's coming from Northwest, direction 335."

"Tell them to contact Georgia 729 right now. They should be 500 miles southwest of us. See if they have also received something."

"Yes, Sir."

Captain Butcher continued examining the map, which he had placed on a small wooden shelf to his right. The seaman's voice was heard again.

"Sir, the Georgia also detected motion on the ground but not the acoustic noise. According to the cross-sections that we have with Georgia's location and data, the epicenter of the blast, or whatever that was, is near us, about thirty-five miles northwest of us. I wrote down the exact location here."

Captain Butcher took the note from the seaman and looked again at the map, searching for the location of the epicenter of that explosion. On its face, the Captain thought, it appears to be an especially powerful explosion, because the ground motion that it created was detected by our sister ship Georgia, which is much farther from us. He picked up the microphone and called out.

"USS 726 Ohio crewmen, this is the Captain speaking. I am reminding you that we are on a level two alert. A few minutes ago, we detected an explosion, probably an exceptional event of unknown magnitude, right at the place in which we would have been right now, had we continued our regular navigation exercise. Communications Officer, transmit a full report on the event immediately to our headquarters back home. When I have further details, I will notify you. USS 726 crew, keep your eyes and ears open. If someone is messing with us, he probably doesn't know what this machine is capable of. Everyone maintain a high state of alert."

Captain Butcher placed the microphone back on its hook and started considering this unusual event. What the hell can this be if it reached all the way to USS 729? There's no chance in the world that the blast was created by standard explosives. What the hell can this be and who planned this and why did it happen in the exact spot that we were supposed to have reached?

As had become his custom, Colonel Yevgeni again assumed command of the discussion. This time, for the first time, Gregory also participated actively.

"There are already reports of a nuclear blast south of the island of Svalbard", Yevgeni opened. "I have no doubt that within a short time, the story will circulate throughout the world. We executed it, it is our responsibility, and our Minister of Defense did not get from us the outcome that he requested. Everybody already knows why it happened, but it's not really going to help if we dwell on the reasons. Our responsibility now is to minimize the damage and help the Minister as much as we can, perhaps even gain some benefit from the event. We must do this within minutes. I don't think we even have as much as half an hour."

"Exactly", replied Gregory, who was showing the first signs of recovery. "But tell me, how can we benefit from such a catastrophe?"

Colonel Yevgeni conferred briefly with his mate Brigadier General

Dimitri, then turned back to the team members, eying Gregory directly.

"In my opinion, we have only one option. We will propose to the Minister that the Soviet Union announce in all mass communication media that we managed to shoot down a cruise missile tipped with a nuclear warhead that was launched by an American bomber over the North Sea. We will say that the missile was on its way to destroy the city and the naval base of Murmansk, and it was only by sheer coincidence that we managed to shoot it down, causing it to explode in the sea."

Gregory stared at Yevgeni, perplexed.

"What's this coincidence that you're talking about?"

"I mean that it should be understood that it was only by a miracle that we managed to save the lives of hundreds of thousands of our citizens. For example, because on that day, our jet fighters were training in the area and they happened to detect the cruise missile and destroy it."

It was Brigadier General Dimitri's turn to speak.

"It's all very well, this idea of a supposed coincidence, but not with airplanes. A cruise missile flies very low and it is difficult to intercept from the air because of the airplane radar's technical limitations. I suggest we change our version and say that one of our battleships detected the missile as it was approaching, and its gunners shot the missile down. By the way, such missiles fly relatively slowly and at low altitude, so it would be possible to down them even with anti-aircraft cannons. Of course, in this explosion, our battleship was also destroyed, and this will be a good opportunity to praise our hero brethren who sacrificed their lives to save several hundred thousand fellow citizens."

"All right, that makes sense", replied Colonel Yevgeni. "Gregory, this is what you should propose to the Minister. I think he will probably adopt this story, especially since right now, we do not have any better alternative to propose."

Gregory rose quickly from his chair and raced from the room. Dimitri turned to Colonel Yevgeni. He wore a serious expression and could not hide his concern.

"This time, my good friend, I'm not so sure that even your good ideas can save our heads."

THE MINISTER OF DEFENSE, MARSHAL BUDARENKO, STORMED into the office suite of the Party's General Secretary. To Svetlana's astonishment, the Minister continued, without stopping, directly into the General Secretary's inner office. Svetlana chased after him, trying to prevent him from entering Secretary Yermolov's room unannounced, but the Minister ignored her pleas and stormed straight into the Secretary's office. Even before Secretary Yermolov could say a word, the Marshal began his speech, remaining on his feet, waving his arms and spouting rebuke.

"Am I mobilizing masses of tanks behind your back? I want to reach the Atlantic coast with my tanks? Now you understand that the Yankee Ambassador, that you like so much, came to pull the wool over your eyes. He came here to lull you. If it weren't for our hero sons on the battleship that, just by chance happened to be in that area, we could now have three hundred thousand burned corpses in Murmansk. We are at war; get this in to your head already. The Yanks are no longer threatening us with war because they have already started it."

The Party General Secretary, the Head of State of the Union of Soviet States, who, just several minutes before, had received word of the nuclear blast in the North Sea, remained silent in his seat. The Minister of Defense took that opportunity to sink his claws deeper into the flesh of the Secretary, who now seemed hesitant and confused.

"You must now come out and address the nation. Our soldiers need to know that they are about to defend the motherland, after we were attacked by the Americans."

The Secretary was trying with all his might to regain his composure in the face of Marshal Budarenko's harsh words and his zeal to exact revenge on the Americans immediately, blow for blow.

"Not one soldier will make any move at the moment to defend the nation on Western European soil", the Secretary said at last. "We will convene, within the hour, an urgent emergency meeting of the senior leadership, and reach decisions. Meanwhile, I will prepare the official announcement to the nation of the attempted attack."

The Secretary's words did not satisfy the Minister's desire for immediate action. He decided to try again.

"Mister Secretary, be specific. This is not an attempted attack but an actual attack. The Americans should not even think that we are hesitating or that we are not determined. Give me the order now to enter the Federal Republic of Germany. Time is not in our favor."

"No order yet", the Secretary replied resolutely, having gained his composure. "I said we'll meet in one hour and make decisions. This meeting is over."

When the Minister left the General Secretary's office, Svetlana hurried into the room. She began apologizing breathlessly for not being able to stop the minister's trajectory into the Secretary's room.

"It's all right", the General Secretary replied, with a bitter smile. "It's not only you. Even I can't stop him."

CHAPTER 13

A PALL OF IMMINENT WAR HUNG IN THE AIR OF THE SITUATION ROOM at the White House in Washington D.C. The high rate and the fast pace of Red Army troop concentrations on the threshold of West Germany had already been interpreted by all intelligence agencies as preparation for an upcoming invasion of West Germany and even beyond.

Seated in the Situation Room were the Chairman of the Joint Chiefs of Staff, General Gorge Abramson; the Chief of Naval Operations, General Tim Ewing; the Chief of Staff of the United States Air Force, General James Cannon; and George Brown, director of the CIA. The door opened and the President of the United States, James Butler, walked into the room, followed by Secretary of Defense Philip Manning. All those present in the room rose to their feet as a mark of respect for the President. The President took his seat at the head of the conference table, swiftly greeted the attendants, and instructed them to take their seats.

James Butler had been President for the past three years. He was the first President in two decades who had not been directly involved in the Vietnam War, which had been traumatic for the American people and for its Presidents. A native of Texas, aged 54 when elected, he was a straight talker, often criticized for his rough, undiplomatic language. At six foot four, the Secret Service agents protecting him had a challenging job. Those selected to serve as his personal guard had to be at least as tall as he was, which gave the group the look of an NBA basketball team on the move. President Butler was a fastidious man who took great care with his appearance at all times. His thick mane was always combed to the right, and he never missed his daily session at the gym.

His term had been relative quiet, both domestically and internationally. On the foreign relations front, his term was free of any notable conflicts. At home, the economy was doing better than average, earning him great public approval. He was married to First Lady Rachel and had two teenage children, a son and a daughter, who lived at the White House with them.

The President scanned the attendees seated around the table. He could easily see the tense atmosphere in the room on the serious, silent faces of the officials sitting around the long rectangular table: the crisis with the Soviet Union, which had started out of the blue, was rapidly escalating.

"I guess we'll be spending some time together in this room in the coming hours and over the next few days", the President opened the emergency meeting. "Secretary Manning has just briefed me on the nuclear explosion in the North Sea. I must tell you that I'm not satisfied with what you've given me so far. You've given me a list of unknowns, including today's unknowns. What exactly am I supposed to do with them? Should I write myself intelligence assessments? Can any one of you stand up and tell me why half of the Red Army is deployed at the East German border? And what the heck was this nuclear explosion in the middle of nowhere?"

The President paused, looking around at the people listening to his every word.

"In addition to all this, two hours ago, the Communist Party General Secretary looked into the face of our Ambassador in Moscow, one might say at the whites of his eyes, saying, 'Tell your President that we will not attack you'. So tell me, what's going on here, for heaven's sake? Secretary Manning, how are the military deployed since the alert was raised to DEFCON 2?"

Defense Secretary Manning glanced quickly at General John Abramson, who nodded to him. The Secretary replied to the President directly.

"Mister President, General John Abramson, who is being constantly briefed from the field, will give an update on the actions carried out so far."

General Abramson rose on his feet and walked to a large map which covered an entire wall.

"Mister President, all of our forces, both here at home and everywhere on the globe, are at the highest alert. This means that all leaves are cancelled and we've started a partial call-up of the reserves. We've stopped all training activities. All the units of our Armed Forces are now filling their personnel vacancies and replenishing their stocks of equipment and ordnance. In Europe, all our forces have left their bases and are deploying in their battle positions on the field. The Strategic Air Command has armed all our four hundred bombers, and they are ready to take off at very short notice. A great part of our ninety-strong assault submarine fleet is en route to their battle and launch positions across the oceans. From this point, we cannot raise our level of readiness any higher. From this point, the next stage is actual combat.

"Regarding the intentions of the Red Army, I will present the view of both the CIA and Military Intelligence. There is a consensus among all of our intelligence agencies. We are united in believing that the present Soviet deployment around East Germany is not intended for handling any internal problem there. This is without doubt a force that was assembled to attack our defense lines in West Germany, and perhaps even to continue deeper into Western Europe. So much for the deployed force and its capabilities. The main question here is intent. Namely, will they really start up their engines and begin moving towards us? Here, one must understand that the Russians know very well what we also know for a fact, that they have a great numerical advantage over us and over NATO in general, in the number of tanks, in the number of armored personnel carriers, in artillery guns and in almost any other parameter. Therefore, they know that the only option that we have for stopping these swarms of armored divisions is solely the use of tactical nuclear weapons. That is also the reason why they have not acted against us until now."

President Butler impatiently interrupted General Abramson, the Commander-in Chief, the most senior officer of the Armed Forces, who reported directly to him.

"I don't understand where you're heading, John. Everything you've said so far is well known. You haven't explained what is different about this week's situation and why they are about to attack now. Why aren't they afraid now, that we'll use nuclear weapons to stop them? Why is this week different from last week? I just don't get it."

A uniformed naval officer entered the room. He saluted the President and requested his permission to deliver an urgent telegram to General Abramson. The Chief of the Joint Staff read the telegram quickly and turned to the President.

"Mister President, we sent several maritime patrol aircraft

and naval vessels to the area east of the nuclear explosion, trying to intercept those responsible for the explosion on their way back to northern Russia", he said, holding the telegram.

"Mister President, I will now read the message that I've just received; it is a message that was broadcast on Radio Moscow five minutes ago. The message begins; The Soviet General Secretary announced on the radio that an American bomber had launched a nuclear cruise missile towards the port city of Murmansk. A Russian destroyer, which happened to be in the area, detected the missile and shot it down with cannon fire, and the missile exploded. All 247 men aboard the destroyer were killed in the blast. They gave their lives to save at least three hundred thousand men and women, children and babies in the city of Murmansk. The Soviet Armed Forces have been placed at the highest alert and they will respond in kind to the American aggression. That's the end of the Radio Moscow message. I assume that in the next few minutes, we'll also receive our intelligence agencies' assessment of this bizarre announcement."

The President hit the table with his fist and leapt to his feet in frustration.

"And this is the General Secretary who looked our Ambassador in the eye and assured him that they wouldn't attack? So what now? Are you going to ask for two more days to analyze this Soviet Secretary's fantasy? Go do your homework. You said there were also some findings in the North Sea relating to the explosion? Then let's meet here in ninety minutes. I also want to hear what our Soviet experts have to say, as I understand that I can't get any answers about their intentions from you military folk."

"Mister President", said CIA director George Brown, "I'd like a private word with you. It won't take more than two minutes."

"Come with me", the President replied curtly and hurried out of the Situation Room, followed by the CIA director. Only the security officials remained in the room, looking forlorn and embarrassed. The President instructed his three Secret Service men to keep their distance.

"Why didn't you speak up in the meeting, George?" asked the President. "Is it possible that even my CIA director doesn't know what the Russians have in store for us?"

"I'll have new information by the next meeting. There are quite a few developments right now, Sir. Mister President I request your special approval in light of this situation, and especially because of the ambiguity surrounding us here, to activate the Raven."

The President mulled this over, running his fingers through his hair.

"As I remember, and correct me if I'm wrong, you told me at the time that the Raven is an extremely senior source at the Kremlin. If we activate the Raven, it may be assumed that the information passed on to us will expose this person. Is that right?"

"That's correct, Mister President. That's why we decided in advance that the Raven should be activated only when we face real danger, and even then, it would require your prior approval."

"Well, I think we have no choice. We are facing real danger, and none of my generals can explain the reason for this danger. Okay, George, activate the Raven."

The President strode away from the CIA director, his security detail rushing to catch up with him.

The Four-Engine Orion P-3 Maritime Patrol Aircraft flew back and forth over the North Sea, northwest of Norway. The pilots had been unequivocally instructed to keep away from the west because of the active radiation which had been detected in the blast area. From time to time, the airborne Geiger counter emitted beeps attesting to the presence of radiation in their immediate surroundings, but these were not at a magnitude that could endanger the air crew.

The navigator held a chart on his knees, on which the search areas were divided into many narrow strips. Since flights like these went back and forth the length of the strips, the pilots dubbed them "ironing missions", as they were similar to the motion of passing an iron over an ironing board. The plane was equipped on both sides with two large observation windows which protruded outwards, like large transparent bubbles. The airborne observer would look through them at the sea, trying to detect suspicious sea vessels.

One of the observers was heard on the pilots' headsets.

"Identifying a wake in the distance at our nine o'clock."

The maritime patrol aircraft sharply banked to the left in a steep dive. Two minutes later, the plane had already made three passes above a medium-size trawler. The observer's voice was heard again on the intercom.

"Okay, I got it on film. It is coming from the exact location of the blast. It could be interesting to ask the crew some questions. By the way, I can't see any fishing nets on its deck, and judging by the black smoke, it's probably racing away to the east at full power."

The plane's captain, experienced in sea patrol missions, needed no further information for all the red lights to go on in his brain. He immediately reported the findings to headquarters. The captain was informed that the battleship USS Iowa was in the area and had already been ordered to intercept the suspicious trawler. Within minutes, the HMS Chester, an old British Royal Navy frigate, which was even nearer to the trawler, was located.

The captain of the maritime patrol aircraft established contact with the British frigate and updated its communications officer with the details of the trawler, its speed, location and course. Then the Orion climbed back to high altitude, as its crew observed the HMS Chester closing the distance to the trawler.

THE CAPTAIN OF THE HMS CHESTER WATCHED THE TRAWLER THROUGH heavy naval binoculars. Judging from its empty decks, the ship seemed deserted, but the great quantity of black smoke pouring from its smokestack confirmed the earlier report that he had received, that the vessel was racing at full power, trying to escape eastwards to the Soviet Union. The captain looked at the name of the ship in large letters on its bow and called out into the microphone over the radio, which was set to the international emergency frequency.

"Zlatoya Klatzo, Zlatoya Klatzo, this is Her Majesty's Ship Chester calling. You are requested to stop for a routine check. Silence your engines; all your crew should come up to the upper deck. Please confirm."

The captain repeated his call several times, but there was no response from the trawler, even when they were cruising parallel to one another at a distance of only 100 meters. The royal frigate's captain pressed the alarm button and the noise of deafening whistles filled the air throughout the ship. Within seconds, scores of the ship's crew were running in every direction to man the heavy gun and machine gun positions, to the takeover team boats, to the fire extinguishing stations and so forth, each to his position and function.

The captain again spoke into the public address microphone.

"Attention, your Captain is speaking. We have a situation here with a vessel that isn't responding on the emergency frequency and is attempting to evade us. Gun crew number two, fire one shell one hundred meters ahead of the trawler's bow...Fire!"

A loud blast shook the frigate, after which the shell exploded just a few meters ahead of the trawler's bow; but it continued on its way, totally disregarding the shelling in its path.

The Chester's captain was again heard on the ship's PA system.

"Takeover Team One and Takeover Team Two, lower boats and prepare to board the trawler. I must remind you that our entire Navy is on supreme alert. Be vigilant and prepare for any eventuality. You are permitted to open fire only if you are fired upon. We will close distance to the trawler and cover you. Go ahead and good luck!"

Two fast rubber assault dinghies, each manned by eight highly skilled and well-equipped Royal Marines, approached the trawler from both sides. The marines attached their boats to the ship's metal body where the height of the deck was lowest, and skillfully threw rope ladders to the decks with anchor-like hooks that caught on the bridge. Within seconds, the first of them climbed, like big cats, over to the deck of the trawler. The captain watched them through his binoculars.

CAPTAIN YASHIN, COMMANDER OF NUCLEAR SUBMARINE K-219, had been observing the trawler through his periscope for quite some time. When he noticed the British frigate approaching the trawler, he called his crew to their battle positions. The pneumatic launch tubes had already been loaded with torpedoes. The submarine crew was awaiting orders.

"Captain", the duty seaman called out beside him, "We are detecting another ship approaching from the south. It's a very large ship, probably a battleship."

Captain Yashin turned his periscope to the south and indeed, the great silhouette of an American battleship was there in all its intimidating glory. He could read its name on its side: BB-61. That is the USS Iowa, the Captain thought, and it's starting to get quite crowded and unpleasant around here. We need to complete our mission and head home. He picked up the microphone.

"Launch Tube One and Launch Tube Two, target ahead, direction one nine five, range two four zero zero. Fire!"

The muffled sound of released pressurized air was heard in the submarine. Through his periscope, Captain Yashin tracked the two torpedoes cutting through the water at a very high speed, leaving two thin white wakes behind them. He decided not to wait until the torpedoes had hit the target, as he figured that he would also hear the explosions underwater. Now we've already been detected, he thought, and they'll come after us, and very soon we'll have depth charges exploding around us. We need to get out of here as soon as possible. He took up the microphone again.

"Dive, dive, dive. Depth two hundred forty, direction zero nine five, full power ahead."

THE TELEPHONE RANG ON THE HMS CHESTER'S COMMAND bridge and the Captain quickly picked it up. A panicky voice was heard on the line.

"Sir, this is the observer. I see a torpedo in the water, racing toward us from east to west. Wait, I see another one. I think they're going to hit the trawler, but I'm not sure. 600 meters, 400… 150."

A powerful explosion was heard and then another, and a huge fireball engulfed the trawler's hull. A shockwave shook the HMS Chester with great force. The Chester's Captain held tightly on to the railing and watched, mesmerized, as the trawler, whose bow seemed to rise skyward, fell back and hit the water with great force. The ship then tilted downwards, bow first, and began sinking rapidly until it was vertical. Within two minutes, only the tip of its stern was visible above water. The ship's propellers, which continued spinning, were now pointed skyward. It was a frightening, chilling sight, yet extraordinarily captivating and powerful. A minute later, the trawler had completely disappeared and a deathly silence returned to the sea.

The HMS Chester's Captain was an old seaman, a veteran of the Second World War. He quickly recovered, and his clear authoritative voice was heard again over the PA system.

"HMS Chester crew, this is the Captain speaking. Lower boats and search for survivors. Damage control team, check for damage and report immediately. The enemy submarine which sank the trawler will be taken care of by our big sister the USS Iowa. Chester crew, we have probably lost some brave men. God save the souls of our heroic brothers."

Two small dinghies searched again and again through the oily waters around the place where the trawler had gone down, between the broken pieces of timber and debris floating in the water. In the distance, the muffled sounds of explosions were heard. These were the depth charges that the USS Iowa was dropping with the intention of hitting the unknown submarine, or at least of causing it enough damage to force it to the surface.

The water was almost frozen and it was clear to everyone that even if some survivors from among the Royal Marines and the trawler's crew had made it out alive, they would not survive in the water for more than a few minutes.

"There's a head!" a voice was heard on one of the two rescue boats, which raced toward it. An athletically-built man was holding on to a piece of lumber floating in the water.

"This one isn't one of ours, and he's as strong as a horse", said one of the rescuers, while pulling the survivor out of the water and into the boat with the help of two of his mates. The survivor seemed to be in shock. He was shivering and his teeth were chattering, making a knocking sound. They laid him down in the center of the boat and covered him with an aluminum thermal blanket to preserve what little remained of his body heat. Despite his condition, he was fully conscious and probably aware of his surroundings.

Within a short time the survivor, supported by two seamen, was brought up to the British frigate and led to the officers' mess. His clothes were removed and he was dressed in a warm, dry uniform. An electric heater was brought and the survivor was served hot tea.

"*Spassiba*", [thank you, in Russian], he whispered.

The frigate's Captain entered the mess hall and looked down at the survivor. He reckoned that despite his condition, the man was bearing up surprisingly well.

"Do you speak English?" the Captain asked him.

"*Nyet, ya gabrit Prusky*", he answered in Russian, saying

that he spoke only Russian.

The phone on the wall rang and one of the seamen answered. He listened and passed the handset to the Captain.

"It's for you, Captain."

The Captain took the handset.

"This is the Captain."

"This is Captain Mitchell, of the USS Iowa. Please accept my condolences. I understand that you've lost some of your men."

"Yes, we have. It seems that all sixteen of our Marines are lost at sea. Thank you for your condolences. Now go on, please."

"We chased after the enemy submarine and dropped several depth charges, but is appears that the enemy wasn't hit and managed to escape to the east. If you have any Russian survivors, we can help. We have an intelligence officer who speaks Russian here on board."

"We have one survivor and he is now…" "You say Russian?"

"Affirmative."

"What's his condition? Can he be questioned?"

"I believe so. He looks pretty tough to me. He was given a change of clothes and some hot tea and he is now recovering. I'm not at all sure that he's just a fisherman."

"OK. Under these circumstances, we don't abide by British etiquette. I promise you that he will very quickly forget he's Mister Tough Guy."

"I'll sail closer to you, and we'll transfer this fisherman to you in an

Omega chair across a wire."

"Hold it, Captain. The Intelligence Officer is right here next to me, and he has two requests. First, tie him to the Omega chair with his hands behind his back so he doesn't try to jump and kill himself. Second, put his original clothes in a plastic bag and send them to us as well."

"No problem, Captain. We'll do all that, and thanks for your help with the submarine."

"Don't mention it. Too bad we didn't hit it. Again, I'm sorry for your loss. We're now approaching your starboard side."

Within minutes, the huge USS Iowa was approaching the British frigate, coming closer and closer. A rope was shot into the water from the Iowa's deck and was collected on the HMS Chester's deck and, fifteen minutes later, a steel-threaded wire was suspended between the two ships.

The Russian survivor was lashed tightly to a chair hanging from an overhead pulley on the cable. Hundreds of seamen stood on the decks of the two ships and watched the Russian survivor being pulled across to the Iowa over the wire.

The Intelligence investigator looked through the Russian's original clothes, and having finished inspecting them, walked to the next room and sat facing the Russian, who was guarded by an armed seaman. He first inspected him visually for quite some time. It was hard not to be impressed by the calm bearing, and strangely enough, even by the confidence displayed by the Russian, considering the circumstances in which he now found himself. The Intelligence officer addressed him in his mother tongue.

"What is your name?" "Vassily."

"Vassily what?" "Vassily."

The interrogator could swear that he noticed a hint of a grin at the corner of the mouth of this Russian, who seemed a hard nut to crack.

"What was your job on the ship? I can see you're not a boy." "Chief Engineer."

"Show me your hands."

The Russian extended his two palms for his interrogator to see.

"And what have you been doing in the past twenty-four hours?"

"We were fishing."

"Tell me about those fish that you caught in these frozen waters. What did you fish? Sardines? Whales? Frozen fillet?"

"I don't know. I am only a Chief Engineer."

"Interesting", the interrogator replied in disdain. "I'm looking at the pictures taken by our maritime patrol airplane, which you must have seen passing above you. It's strange; there are no fishing nets on the deck. Maybe you were fishing with those long antennas that covered your entire ship? I hear about fisherman that use explosives for fishing, even though it's illegal, but fishing with a nuclear bomb? Haven't you gotten it mixed up? Do you agree with me that maybe you went overboard just a little bit?"

The Russian survivor kept quiet and displayed no emotion.

"Now tell me, what's this big thing covered with a tarp in the middle of the ship? Maybe that's where you stored all your fishing nets? No? To me it looks rather like a tank or a self-propelled gun. Maybe it caused your ship to sink to the bottom of the ocean like a stone after you were hit by the torpedo – the tank or the gun rolled forward and its weight caused the ship to stand on its nose and to plunge to the bottom. There's another thing I want to ask you, just out of curiosity. Tell me, do all fishermen in Russia have Soviet Navy storm coats?"

The interrogator looked at the Russian's face and thought he noticed some signs of uneasiness, but he was not sure of it, and he decided to increase his subtle pressure on the Russian.

"Listen up. This was only the foreplay, and our foreplay ends now. I know you are an officer in the Red Army. As one officer to another, I will share with you some important information. You were sunk by two torpedoes, and these torpedoes were fired by your own nuclear submarine K-219. Now, isn't this obvious to you? Would it make sense for us to sink you before we found out what you have on board and while we had sixteen British Marines on your deck? Why do I have a strange feeling that you know this submarine, and I have a hunch that you also know its Captain personally? You left from the same port, right? When we caught you, you were trying to run towards Murmansk. Now tell me, are you stupid? Don't you realize that this submarine was ordered by your own commanding officers to sink you, in order to silence you forever?"

The Russian survivor struggled valiantly to maintain his composure, but then the interrogator hit him with the final blow.

"Now you listen very carefully. I will eventually get from you everything that I want to hear. We are on supreme alert, and that definitely justifies special treatment. Strike that, violent treatment! Very violent! Later on, just because I'm humane, I will return you to the Soviet Union. This time, they won't waste a torpedo on you – they'll simply finish you off with their bare hands."

The interrogator stopped for several seconds, as if to ensure that his words had indeed penetrated the stoic Russian's head.

"You know what? I'll go further, much further. You cooperate with me and I'll arrange political asylum for you in the United States. I'm giving you five minutes to think over my proposal, which will expire five minutes from now."

The American rose, turned his back on the Russian and left the room. Outside, he lit a cigarette and kept looking at his watch. Five minutes later, the interrogator returned to the room and sat just a few centimeters from the Russian survivor's face. He looked at his watch.

"Your five minutes are up. Did you want to tell me something?"

The Russian maintained his calm expression. Now, he looked his interrogator straight in the eye, and in a diametrical change of roles, it was the American who waited in suspense for the Russian's answer. Will he take me up on my offer, he thought, or will he keep silent?

CHAPTER 14

Party general secretary Vladimir Petrovich Yermolov looked at his watch.

"We have exactly ten minutes before we start the emergency meeting of the inner circle leadership. Speak up."

The Chief of the KGB placed a file of papers on the table and scanned a few of them quickly.

"Mister General Secretary. This is the report on everything that Minister Marshal Budarenko has been doing in the past ten days."

The Party Secretary seemed surprised. His eyebrows rose when he took the papers in his hands.

"I don't understand. I asked you this morning to follow him and you give me material from ten days back? Wait - actually, I do understand.

You've been following him all year. Does this mean that you're also following me?"

The KGB chief was surprised by the General Secretary's direct question, but he composed himself quickly.

"You, Sir, Mister General Secretary, we protect."

The General Secretary lifted his gaze from the papers he was holding and looked directly into the eyes of his subordinate.

"Protect? Well, so be it. It's just semantics. By the way, as

I know myself, I assume that whoever follows me is bored most of the time. Now, I don't have time to read all these papers. Give me the bottom line. Have you found something irregular?"

"In general, Marshal Budarenko spends most of his time in meetings and discussions with the commanders of our Armed Forces, especially those dealing with logistics, and of course, this is related to the mobilization of our forces to the west of the country."

"Well, that's obvious", the General Secretary said impatiently.

"True, Mister General Secretary, but we have nevertheless detected some irregular activity, and we don't exactly understand its significance at the moment. There's a top secret Military Intelligence base outside of Moscow, and the Minister has made a few visits there in the past few days. Compartmentalization there is so severe, that it is difficult for us to decipher the activity. Nevertheless, we were able to detect a strange team of six senior officers who were collected there from various seemingly unrelated places, and I say 'seemingly', as there seems to be no prior relationship whatsoever between them. What we have found so far is that they left a few days ago for the naval base in Murmansk and then returned from there three days later. One of them, by the way, remained in Murmansk."

The Party General Secretary was trying to understand the meaning of all this. He tapped the table with his fingers.

"Murmansk, you say? That is the city that was saved today from that American nuclear missile. But I don't see any relation between these events. You know who that officer is who stayed in Murmansk?"

"Yes, Sir. He is a Colonel of Kazakh origin." "And what does he know? What can he do?" "His expertise is explosives and ordnance."

The Party General Secretary dismissed this information with a wave.

"Well, if we check every military man, in the end we'll find out that he's connected to things that explode and kill, right?"

"Yes Mister General Secretary. This Colonel, whose name, by the way, is Nazarbayev, is not 'in the end', but rather from the beginning. He is perhaps the Red Army's top explosives and ordnance expert."

"Well, this is good. Continue following and keep me updated. I must go to the meeting now."

IN ONE OF THE KREMLIN'S CONFERENCE ROOMS, ALL THE OFFICERS and officials of the highest political and military echelons in the Soviet Union were gathered for an emergency meeting. The Minister of Defense, Marshal Budarenko, was surrounded by many of these, and he seemed to enjoy answering their questions and being the center of attention.

The General Secretary of the Communist Party entered the room quickly. All those present hurried to their seats and remained standing until their leader took his seat. He watched them from his chair for a moment before motioning to them to sit down. He began speaking immediately.

"This meeting will be brief. We shall make operational decisions and each of you will leave at once for his post to execute his mission. This morning, an American cruise missile with a nuclear warhead was launched towards our city of Murmansk. Had it not been for our 247 sons who sacrificed their lives on one of our naval ships, Murmansk would have been destroyed. A few minutes ago, I received a report that two warships, one British and one American, aggressively stopped an innocent fishing boat of ours and then sank it together with its crew. I don't understand where these Americans are heading with this. On one hand, one such missile is not just a declaration of war – it is actual war, for all intents and purposes. On the other hand, there's been no further activity on their part."

"Mister General Secretary, for the time being, no further activity", thundered the voice of the Minister of Defense.

"True, Marshal. For the time being, there's been no activity. But when one starts a war, at least as far as I know, one doesn't execute a single local, limited act, as severe as it may be, and then go to sleep. Therefore, for me, what has happened up till now is unequivocal, and it's clear to me that we must respond. We cannot, and shall not, hold back. However, our response must be measured, so that our enemy will accept it without responding and putting us on a path of no return. This means that we won't seek an all-out nuclear confrontation. I don't know exactly how this can be done; how you can walk in the rain without getting wet. That is why you are here, and I seek your opinion. It's crucial to me that at such a critical moment in our nation's history, there isn't even one person among you here in this room that has something to say or propose and is afraid to say it, preferring to keep his ideas to himself. If I am not clear enough, then I order each one of you to speak his mind."

To everyone's surprise, it was the Commander of the Air Force, General Alexander Mikhailov, who raised his hand and requested to speak. This was irregular, as the ethics of military conduct in the Soviet Armed Forces dictated that the Commander of the Air Force should ask for permission to speak only after his superior, the Minister of Defense, had had his say.

Marshal Budarenko now looked as though, if he had a sword in his hand, he would decapitate the Air Force chief on the spot. His face became red and swollen and his eyes burned with wrath at his uncouth top airman. The Party General Secretary, while noting his Minister's response, nevertheless decided to let the general speak.

"Mister General Secretary Yermolov and Minister Marshal Budarenko, there is one point, the significance of which is vague. The magnitude of the blast in the North Sea was estimated by us to be 0.1 megaton. This is a much smaller magnitude than the standard nuclear missile warheads the Americans usually carry. It's strange that precisely when attacking a real target, they used a much smaller warhead."

"What are you hinting at, General?" the Party General Secretary asked. "That this is an action that happened inadvertently because of an error or failure in the system, and perhaps that could explain why there's no continuation of their hostilities?"

"I'd hesitate to say this, Mister General Secretary, even though accidents do happen. And we should remember that in this very area, the Americans drill year-round for assaulting us with nuclear weapons. By the way, in the winter of 1968, in Greenland, which is not very far from this morning's blast site, an American B-52 bomber crashed with four nuclear bombs on board. The bombs went off, but no nuclear explosion occurred because they were not armed."

The Party Secretary looked now at the Minister of Defense who was continuing his histrionics from his chair and shooting threatening looks at the Air Force commander.

"Minister of Defense, I want to hear your opinion of the issue raised by the Commander of the Air Force."

The Minister, who had not yet regained his composure, shifted his smoldering gaze from the officer to the General Secretary.

"Mister General Secretary, sometimes I can't explain the *bardak* in the Air Force under General Mikhailov", the Minister said, using the Russian word for bordello. "Is he trying to explain what happens in the American Air Force? General Mikhailov's remark contains an obvious inherent contradiction. The bombs of the plane that crashed thirteen years ago in Greenland were not armed, and they had never been armed in their other training missions. This morning, the missile exploded only because it was armed. The person who decides whether to arm such a missile is not the ordnance NCO of the bomber which launches that missile. This is an order that comes down only from above, from the highest authority. Is that correct, General Mikhailov?"

The Minister didn't wait for the Air Force Commander's reply, and continued with great pathos.

"If you walk in the rain, you get wet, Mister Secretary. It's as simple as that. In my opinion, there is no continuation of American hostilities at the moment, but only because they're waiting in fear to see our response. They know that we'll respond, but they don't know how and where. Our forces in the West are prepared and they expect you, Mister General Secretary, to give them the order. We must now enter the German Democratic Republic and continue on from there, into the German Federal Republic."

The Party General Secretary remembered, in great detail, the difficult conversation he had had with his Minister of

Defense just a few hours ago. He decided to lead him into a trap.

"I understand you, Marshal. If I give you a green light now to enter the Democratic Republic, how long would it take you to cross the border into the Federal Republic? The forces you have mobilized there are only sufficient for handling civil obedience, not a war with NATO. Am I correct, Marshal Budarenko?"

But an old war fox like Marshal Budarenko would not step on a mine as crude as this, and indeed he skipped over it casually.

"Mister General Secretary, regarding your first question, our forces can roll through the Democratic Republic within 36 to 48 hours, and then start crossing the border into the Federal Republic. Regarding your first question, it is obvious that I still don't have the order of battle I wish to have, but we'll breach their defenses with what we have, and within another forty-eight hours, we'll push everything we can into there."

The Party General Secretary nodded as if approving his Minister's explanation. This son of a gun has already mobilized enough forces to conquer almost all of Western Europe, the Party General Secretary thought. Is he going to request an approval for general mobilization now?

"Marshal Budarenko", the General Secretary said in a steady, authoritative voice. "Move your forces into the German Democratic Republic, and when you reach the border with the Federal Republic, breach the border only in the northern sector."

The General Secretary pulled a piece of paper out of his pocket and studied it.

"You will get to the Weser River in the section from the city of Bremen in the North, to the city of Göttingen in the South. But approval to cross this river will be given only here in this room and in this forum, after we see the enemy's response. Is everything clear so far, Marshal Budarenko?"

"Yes, Mister General Secretary. Everything is clear."

PRESIDENT JAMES BUTLER ENTERED THE WHITE HOUSE SIT-UATION ROOM. His concern was apparent, and he spoke at once.

"I hope you've all updated and collected all the missing data so you can explain it to me, and give me a better understanding of the situation. Maybe now I can finally get the point of what these Russians are preparing for us."

President Butler had a unique and somewhat unorthodox approach toward his senior staff and advisers in emergencies that required deliberations and decision-making of the highest order. Unlike his manner on less eventful days, when the President addressed them by their first names, this time he addressed them by their official titles, as if stressing their responsibility to the American people, and to him personally.

"Secretary of Defense Manning, please speak now, or perhaps you prefer that Chairman of the Joint Chiefs of Staff General Abramson continue from where he stopped the last time we met?"

"Mister President, there have now been quite a few developments, especially in the North Sea, and General Abramson has the details. Therefore, I request that he brief you on the present situation."

The President turned to the Chairman of the Joint Chiefs of Staff.

"Well, General, what's new? Speak up."

General Abramson stood up and walked to the chart on the wall.

"Mister President, a short while ago, the crew of a British frigate intercepted a suspicious Russian trawler sailing at full power from the area of the blast towards their major naval base in Murmansk."

"And what was suspect about this trawler?" the President asked.

"Its direction indicated that it was coming from the area of the blast, so it seemed to be involved in that matter. In addition, this fishing vessel had no fishing nets and no other fishing equipment. Our intelligence photographed it from the air, and the pictures showed that it was equipped with many antennas, unlike a typical fishing vessel. Moreover, in the middle of the deck, there was a large object concealed with a tarp. Our intelligence analysts claim that it could be a tank or a self-propelled artillery gun."

The President abruptly interrupted General Abramson

"I don't understand what you're talking about, General. You say 'suspicious', 'our analysts', 'maybe a tank, may be a gun'. Is this a quiz? You said the British warship intercepted the trawler. Since when do the British hide information from us? Besides, even I know that the Soviets camouflage their surveillance ships as fishing vessels. This isn't new to us, is it?"

"I'm sorry, Mister President, my mistake", the General replied apologetically. "What I didn't say was that when a takeover team boarded the trawler, a Russian submarine launched a torpedo at the trawler, and the boat sank, together with the British Marines."

"Now I get it. How many British soldiers were there?" "Two teams. Sixteen Marines, Sir. All lost at sea." "And the Russian crew? Are they all gone?"

"We received a report just before we came here, from our own USS Iowa, which is also in the area, saying that there is one Russian survivor. He's in good condition and the British, who fished him out of the water, agreed to transfer him to the Iowa for questioning. We have a Russian-speaking interrogator there, so we should know more very soon."

The President turned to his aide seated behind his chair.

"Since this is an emergency, tell the Iowa that they have my approval to skin this Russian alive if need be, if it gets him to start talking, and pretty damn quickly."

"Yes, Mister President", the aide said, and hurried out of the room.

"Now go on, General."

"It stands to reason that this vessel was in the vicinity of the event when it took place, and that it even participated in creating the event. The fact that a Russian submarine followed the trawler and blasted it to smithereens just as the British were boarding it, proves that they had a very good reason to make this vessel disappear, and especially to silence the crew permanently. What we have so far is that the Russian survivor is in good condition and he was wearing a Russian Navy coat. And several minutes ago, Radio Moscow reported that, following the so-called American aggression of this morning, British and American warships sank a Russian trawler in the North Sea."

President Butler nodded and turned to his Secretary of Defense, Mr. Manning.

"After the nuclear missile that they attributed to us, this is really quite benign. I want us to move forward. What's our intelligence assessment regarding the nuclear explosion and the vast forces that they're deploying around East Germany?"

"Mister President, I'll get straight to the point. Our intelligence community all agree that they plan to attack us in the near future in Europe, and more precisely, in West Germany. There are several obvious reasons. The forces they've mobilized so far are several times larger than what they need to suppress the insurgency in East Germany. Our assessment is that since it is impossible to conceal the presence of all the divisions that have been concentrated there, but not the reason for which they are concentrated there, they decided to execute a small nuclear explosion that would achieve two goals, a small one and a big one. The small goal is to divert the world's attention, and ours, from the area of potential conflict in the German Democratic Republic to another, more remote region. The other goal, which is the primary one in our opinion, is to frame us, to attribute to us an attempt to annihilate a large city, Murmansk, with a nuclear weapon, thereby justifying their invasion of West Germany as a legitimate punitive action. They estimate that even then, we would not be eager to use tactical nuclear weapons to stop the advance of the massed Soviet armor."

President Butler thought to himself for a moment, and then addressed Secretary of Defense Manning again.

"This is definitely an analysis that I can accept. But then, what do you think the motive is for this insanity by these goddamn Communists?"

"Mister President, there is no question here that they want to save their homeland. That's exactly how they see it. We have indications that even in the Soviet Union itself, some unrest has started among some restive labor unions and industrial complexes. In their view, all evil and fermentation originates in the free states of Western Europe, and therefore, in order to nip this agitation and insurrection in the bud, they must neutralize those states. They also believe that by doing this they can put a stop to outside agitation, and also, judging from history, when the motherland is at war against an external enemy, the whole nation unites behind the regime and its leaders. As they see it, it's like killing two birds with one stone."

A junior naval officer entered the room. He saluted, and General Abramson snatched from his hand, almost violently, a sheet of paper fresh from the teleprinter. The Admiral read it intently.

"What is it, General? Has the Russian fishermen started talking?"

"No, Sir", General Abramson replied, still reading the paper. "I'm afraid, Sir, that our time is running out. Both our Intelligence and our allies in West German Intelligence are detecting a general rush of activity over the radio networks in the past half hour, unprecedented in its scope, to hundreds of Soviet troops, especially the armored divisions. It appears that they are receiving orders to move forward."

A stunned silence descended upon the Situation Room.

"Mister Manning, Secretary of Defense", President Butler said softly in a subdued voice that was nonetheless sharply authoritative. "The Reds are waging war and we are still talking ourselves to death here. I want to hear plans of action right now. But first of all, General", he turned to the Chairman of the Chiefs of Staff, "If they start moving now, how long will it take them to reach the antitank positions between the Germanys?"

"Mister President, it will take them a day and a half, maybe two days at most. In East Germany, they are on friendly territory, all their tanks can move freely on the highways, just like in a military parade. The only thing that can slow them down, in my opinion, is traffic congestion. Nothing else".

The President turned to his aide, who had returned to the Situation Room.

"Secretary of State Peter Perry is sitting outside with the Russian ambassador. Tell Secretary Perry to get rid of the Russian and come here at once."

The aide hurried out of the room.

A minute later, the aide returned with the Secretary of State in tow.

"Sit down, please", the President ordered the Secretary. "Mister President, the Russian Ambassador said that..." The President interrupted him unceremoniously.

"This communist's lies don't interest me right now", said the President.

The Secretary of State was astounded. He had never been treated like this by the President and had never seen him in such a combative mood. The President disregarded his Secretary's offended expression and went on.

"Mister Perry, half an hour ago, the Red Army's masses of tanks and armored personnel carriers started their engines and are moving towards us. The time for diplomacy is over and the time for action has begun. Within thirty-six hours we will be at war against enormous numbers of tanks that can flood the European continent in a few days. I want you to be an active participant in the decisions that we will be taking now."

Secretary Perry nodded, acknowledging the gravity of the situation. The President quickly turned to the Secretary of Defense.

"Secretary Manning, what can we do now except sit on our hands waiting for them to overrun us?"

"Mister President, there are quite a few targets that we can attack in

East Germany, but we will then be perceived as the belligerent party".

"I can live with that", the President replied irritably. "We are at a huge numerical disadvantage against their tanks. So I understand that you're referring to an aerial assault, right?"

"Yes, Sir. We have qualitative superiority in the air, in both aircraft and ordnance."

The President now turned to the Chief of Staff of the Air Force, General James Cannon.

"All our planes are armed and ready. What can we achieve by attacking, General?"

"Mister President, we are in the middle of winter, so it's almost impossible to operate at night. In addition, East Germany has the densest and most effective anti-aircraft array in the world with thousands of antiaircraft missiles in almost one hundred batteries. This is sure to cause us significant losses."

"I didn't ask about losses, General", the President rumbled. "If they breach the West German border, there will be many more losses. What can you do?"

"Mister President, we have several squadrons of A-10 attack aircraft which are highly effective tank hunters. They are very efficient and can work at low altitude, and therefore can't fall prey to most of their antiaircraft missiles. Recent reports of the Soviet inventory at the front mentioned 30,000 tanks; if that is so, we can delay their advance but not much else. We can also attack roads and bridges. We can gain around sixteen to eighteen hours."

The President looked into the faces of each of those present.

"Is everybody in agreement with the General? If so, then all we have to do now, in your opinion, is to sit on our fat asses and wait for the swarms of tanks to flood our forces and our allies?"

The Situation Room fell into absolute silence. Nobody spoke. The President got to his feet and started pacing around the conference table, his subordinates following him with their eyes.

"White House Chief of Staff!" "Yes, Mister President."

"Go out now, please, and tell the Press Secretary to call an emergency press conference. Have them wait for me in the press room and I'll get there in a few minutes."

The Secretary of State, like the rest of his colleagues in the room, had no idea what the President was plotting, but unlike his colleagues, he asked the President directly.

"Mister President, what are you going to tell the nation?" "Lies. Simply lie to them."

"What, Mister President? I don't understand." "You will soon understand, as will everyone else."

The President turned to George Brown, the CIA Director.

"Are you with us? Are you sure? Again, you are not speaking. Does the Central Intelligence Agency have nothing to say? Have you contacted our friend in Moscow?"

"Mister President, I am just as worried that our military options, outside of launching tactical nuclear weapons, are very limited. Regarding that source, a directive has gone out and we will soon be getting information."

"Let me correct you", the President replied. "Our options, outside of activating tactical nuclear weapons, are not limited; they are nonexistent. I have a question for you, as an intelligence expert. If we now send a message to all our commands, including our headquarters in Germany, and this communication must reach the last tactical missile battery in Germany, what are the chances of the Russians intercepting and deciphering the message, and how long will it take them?"

All eyes were on the CIA director.

"Mister President, I am sorry to say that they have incredible capabilities in this area, even though we code our messages, of course."

The President did not waste time waiting for the CIA Director to finish his words.

"In this case, that I have in mind, it could be an advantage. You make sure this communication is coded, but not too heavily. I want them to decipher it is soon as possible. If it weren't to arouse suspicions, I would ask you to transmit the message as is. Now carry on, Mister Director".

"Mister President, if it is not coded heavily, they will decipher it within half an hour, even twice over."

"Hold on, I don't understand. What do you mean by half an hour twice over? Do you mean a quarter of an hour?"

"No, Mister President, sorry I wasn't clear. I meant to say that when the message leaves the Pentagon, their experts in the Russian Embassy here will have deciphered it. If not, then Russian Intelligence will definitely decipher it when it reaches Germany."

The President of the United States, the Commander in Chief, rubbed his fingers slowly over his cheek.

"Since you've left me no choice and have given me no useful, effective military option, and since within a day or two we will probably be in the middle of a war, then all I have left to do is gamble. I've just been thinking over a pretty weird idea, but the more I think of it, the more I like it.

"I want to play them on two playing fields at the same time; exactly as they are playing with us, with force on the German front and with deceit in the North Sea. I'm going to play the Russians at their own game, according to their rules – exactly. I have no doubt that it will cause them serious confusion, which may expose their real intentions."

Secretary Perry, as well as Secretary Manning, seemed puzzled.

"Mister President", said the Secretary of State. "I don't get it. What are you going to do?"

"I'll explain. In field number one, I want to show them an iron fist, to make them think that I'm eager to use the opportunity that they have given me to blast their forces. You two", the President looked at his Secretary of Defense and then at the CIA director, who were anxious to hear the rest of the President's plan.

"You two will issue a directive, relaying a fictitious order from me as Commander in Chief of the United States Armed Forces. In this message, I will order that all our tactical nuclear weapons fire their nuclear warheads the minute the Soviet forces cross a certain line in East Germany, which I will show you now."

President Butler stood up and turned to the large map on the wall behind his chair. He studied the map briefly, then placed his finger on a spot on it, and, still holding his finger there, he turned his head back to his audience.

"Write this down. That line is twelve longitude, north of the city of Rostock and then along the river Elbe. Once the first Soviet tanks cross that line, the order is to fire at will. This order must not be ambiguous and cannot be interpreted in any other way. The Soviets will understand that I am determined to destroy their armor while it is still on East German territory."

The President looked at the officials around the table to see if everyone was following.

"Is it clear so far?"

"Yes, Mister President", the Defense Secretary and the CIA director replied almost in unison.

"Now, let's go to the other game on the other field, which is the public one. There I will play the exact opposite. There I will be the purest nun, from the most sacred convent, a Mother Theresa. I will soon hold a press conference that will open with an address to the nation. I'll begin with a heartfelt apology and condolences to the Soviet nation on the death of their seamen in the explosion in the North Sea. I will announce that the government of the United States has decided to compensate the families of the dead in dollars. I'll explain to them that a malfunction occurred in one of our strategic bombers, which was on a training mission, carrying missiles made for practice and therefore, with relatively small warheads. Here I need your help, Mister Commander of the Air Force. Please give me a scenario that may explain why such a missile would be launched from a bomber."

The Commanding Officer of the Air Force thought this over.

"Mister President, it could be an extremely rare coincidence where the pilot, mistakenly and contrary to standing orders, pressed the button of an electrical system in the middle of a powerful thunderstorm. The bomber was charged with such an amount of static electricity that it caused an electrical short, resulting in a spontaneous missile launch. We can also add that this is the first time we were aware of such a problem, and that of course, we are investigating etc. etc."

"Good for you, General. Finally, you are creative", the President teased his Air Force Chief.

"Mister President", the Commander of the Air Force continued, pointedly ignoring the President's implied rebuke. "Perhaps we can go another step forward and assume full responsibility for the entire event, from beginning to end. That is, we can say that the missile exploded due to a self-destruct order that we radioed to it in order to prevent a catastrophe in Russia. This way, they will understand that the missile would not have continued to Murmansk in any case, and of course, we will voice our regrets that a Russian Navy vessel happened to be in the area of the explosion."

The President took a few seconds to collect his thoughts before he responded to the Air Force General. His head leaned on his fists and his forehead was furrowed.

"I will indeed use the description of the incident as you recommend, as well as the self-destruct at our initiative. After all, it makes sense.

However, I don't want in any way to contradict their version and suggest that they are liars. As I've already said, I'm going to play along with their game. I can't wait to see their faces over there in the Kremlin when they hear my speech. I think it will cause them some confusion and everything will be open to question. From that moment, they'll start suspecting us and what we have in store for them. Add to this the order to launch nuclear missiles without deliberation on anyone daring to cross the 12th Longitudinal, and the confusion in the Kremlin will be complete."

President Butler leaned back in his chair a little smugly,

folding his arms behind his head.

"Well, gentlemen, what do you think? Secretary Perry?"

"Mister President, even if we did have an implementable military option, I have a feeling that your plan would lead to a much better outcome."

"Mister President", this time it was the CIA director. "I think that this is an excellent idea that could confuse them and cast doubts on their course of action so far. They won't understand why we've adopted their false version regarding the cruise missile, and therefore will also have a hard time understanding what our follow-up plans are."

President Butler smiled slightly, for the first time in many days. He turned to his spy chief.

"So, when I retire, can you get me a job with your agency?"

The director smiled.

"Of course, Mister President, I will be delighted, even though I'm sure that you will be offered more senior positions with better compensation."

"Well, we've got a war to run. I'm going to the press room. Keep your fingers crossed for me, and for the American people."

The President rose to his feet and strode out of the room.

CHAPTER 15

THE RED ARMY'S GENERAL STAFF HEADQUARTERS WAS housed in a huge, imposing building on the Moskva River in Moscow's Khamovniki district. The white building was dubbed by many, though not in public, "the Russian Pentagon". The Minister of Defense, Marshal Budarenko, was sitting several floors below ground level, in the war room complex. This was a world in itself, now buzzing with activity. Dozens of officers and soldiers moved around the spacious halls in a frenzy. A large, low table in the center of the room held a map of the European continent. Small wooden models, especially of tanks, most of them blue and the others red, were scattered around the map. Soldiers surrounded the table holding what looked like pool table cue sticks, moving the small models around the map. Most of the tank models were concentrated in the area on the table representing Poland and the two Germanys, blue against red.

The Minister of Defense sat in his office on the second floor with a glass wall which afforded him a commanding view of the large, spacious control table. His military adjutant sat next to him, passing to him, from time to time, dispatches received from the front by a teleprinter in the next room. Most of the dispatches were reports concerning problems or requests from various units in the field, especially regarding supplies of fuel and ammunition. Only two hours before, the Minister of Defense had ordered all the Soviet ground forces stationed in Poland to move west into the territory of the German Democratic Republic. The first tank units had already crossed the border, and so far, no resistance by the German civilian population or the East German army had been recorded. The maneuver was going ahead without incident. It is still too early to draw conclusions, the Minister thought to himself, but so far the reports have been encouraging. If it goes on like this, we can cross the border between the Germanys in just over 24 hours.

The Minister focused his gaze on the large control table on the floor below. A dense concentration of little wooden tanks lined the central route leading to Berlin. North of it, an even larger force was concentrated in the area of the city of Szczecin in Poland, and an arrow pointed towards the large port city of Hamburg. From the concentration point of the third, southernmost force, an arrow pointed towards three cities in West Germany: Leipzig, Dessau and Halle.

The Minister was feeling elated by the show of force. He turned to his adjutant.

"It's amazing how everything is falling into place without incident. This is not something that's ever been done before – I'm moving the largest armored force here that the world has ever known. You may be too young to know, but six thousand tanks took part in the great battle of Kursk in 1943, and the battle of Kursk was considered – until today – the biggest concentration of armor in history. That was true up until two hours ago. I am now moving almost thirty thousand tanks into battle. Do you understand what is happening here? It's five times more than all the forces fighting in Kursk!"

"Mister Minister, your name will be etched in golden letters in the books of military history, and all military academies will teach your maneuver. This is further proof of what you have always said: that it all begins and ends with planning. When planning is done with great care to the smallest details, then in the field, everything happens without incident."

The adjutant glanced at Marshal Budarenko, trying to assess the

Minister's satisfaction with the flattery he had just been served, but the Minister's face remained without expression. A bundle of telegrams was brought into the room and the adjutant started sorting them.

"Mister Minister, updates are beginning to arrive from our forces about their advance into the German Democratic Republic. At the moment, the northern force is the farthest west. By the way, we've also just received a translation of the Address to the Nation by the President of the United States."

"What? When did he speak? What does he have to say after trying to destroy the city of Murmansk? Did this criminal beg for forgiveness?"

A disparaging smile spread from ear to ear on the Minister's face. He looked through the window to the large table below him.

"It's too bad I can't show him that table down there, but his soldiers will soon see this in action, or - how do they say it in English? - they will see this LIVE!"

"Mister Minister", the adjutant spoke again. "He actually apologized." "What? What are you talking about? Who apologized?"

"The American President Butler. He even offered monetary compensation to the families of the seamen who died on our battleship."

The Minister of Defense savagely snatched the paper from his adjutant's hand. He read the contents over and over, unable to believe his eyes.

How can that be? He thought to himself. Now he wasn't elated, but rather concerned. His head was spinning with thoughts and pictures. Maybe they're deterred by the vast forces that we have concentrated against them, he thought, and in order to appease us, they're willing to go along with our story and even to assume responsibility for the missile that blew up; anything to prevent our advance. Yes, that's probably the logical explanation for what the President said, the Minister reasoned to himself with satisfaction. I seem to have managed to bring these arrogant Americans down to their knees, very low to their knees.

A young officer entered the room and put a sealed envelope into the hands of the Minister's adjutant.

"This is addressed to you personally, Mister Minister", the adjutant said, handing the envelope to the Minister.

Marshal Budarenko took the envelope, broke the seal, and read the content of the message, which was marked in large letters: TOP SECRET – SENSITIVE – ADDRESSEE ONLY. The Minister finished reading the dispatch and suddenly seemed like a changed man. He looked very pale, beads of sweat appeared on his forehead and his heart beat rapidly. He tried with all his might to calm himself, as if he were on the battlefield. He read the dispatch again, and this time the list of the other recipients at the foot of the letter caught his eye. First on the list was the Party General Secretary. Budarenko clamped his hand on the shoulder of his adjutant, who looked at him in surprise.

"Run out now and halt the distribution of this message. It is false, it is deceit. No one should get it, not even the Party General Secretary. Do you understand? Now run."

The adjutant rushed out. The Minister lifted the receiver of the red telephone near him.

"Get me Gregory Livkin from Special Forces Base 8749 – at once!"

A few seconds passed, then Gregory's voice came on the line.

"Mister Minister, Gregory Livkin speaking. How can I be of service, Sir?"

"I want to speak with Colonel Yevgeni at once." "Yes, Minister, immediately."

Yevgeni came on the line.

"Mister Minister. This is Colonel Yevgeni speaking."

"Listen up, Colonel. Apparently your idea with the cruise missile and its interception was so good that even the Americans bought it."

"Yes, Minister. Actually, the idea was Brigadier General Dimitri's. I only supported it. But excuse me, Minister, I don't understand what you meant about the Americans."

"The American President spoke a few minutes ago to his nation, but he was really speaking to us. He apologized for launching the missile with the bomb and explained that it was done in error, and he even offered to pay compensation to the families of our dead seamen. How do you explain this, Colonel?"

There was a silence on the other end, perhaps a moment too long. The

Minister of Defense was now impatient and angry.

"Why are you keeping your mouth shut, Colonel? Did you swallow your tongue?"

"Sorry, Minister. I was trying to think of the reasons. In my opinion, they're feeling pressured by the amount of armor that you mobilized against them. They know that they don't have the conventional capacity to stop such numbers of tanks. Therefore, in an attempt to stop them, they are willing to accept any humiliation, even to assume responsibility for the event in the North Sea. That is my opinion, Mister Minister."

"Colonel Yevgeni, this is also what I thought until five minutes ago."

"And what happened five minutes ago, Mister Minister, that changed your mind?"

"I got a telegram from our Intelligence people who intercepted a radio directive in which the American President, as Commander in Chief of the Armed forces, instructs his military to launch tactical nuclear missiles if our tanks move across the Twelfth longitudinal, which is more or less the Elbe River in the German Democratic Republic. What do you have to say to that, Colonel?"

"Mister Minister, may I ask you first how our Intelligence analysts interpret this information?"

"Listen well, Colonel. I don't care what they think. I want to hear a neutral assessment from you, without your being influenced by what they say. There was a reason I selected you for the team, and you've even proved to me here and there in the past few days that I wasn't wrong."

"Thank you, Mister Minister", Yevgeni replied, hiding a shy smile. "I am going over several possibilities."

"Well, Colonel, do it quickly. I don't have time to waste. Speak." "Mister Minister, I believe that what you thought until five minutes ago was correct, and is still valid. In my opinion, the Americans can read their situation very well and they've decided to gamble, hoping it might cause you some confusion. In my estimation, they won't use tactical nuclear weapons, certainly not in the first stage of the war. I think that the President's order to the missile batteries is fictitious and deceitful and they wanted us to intercept it, have second thoughts, and stop the tanks."

"I think so too", replied Marshal Budarenko. "Good, Colonel, thank you."

Colonel Yevgeni froze. He had never heard the word "thank you" leave the lips of this tough, highly decorated Marshal, whose looming, bullying presence had intimidated many good people. In a split-second decision, Yevgeni addressed the Minister again.

"Mister Minister, with your permission, I'd like to tell you something else, and I apologize in advance if I touch a sensitive point. Do I have your permission to speak?"

"Yes, speak, but do it quickly."

"I don't think it's likely, but we must also consider another possibility. It may be that the Americans are aware of your exact plans and that the Party General Secretary is not privy to the matter. I mean to say that even General Secretary Yermolov is certain that the Americans launched the missile, and now they are apologizing, but also threatening that if our tanks continue to move westward, they will respond with nuclear force. Maybe they hope that this will convince the Secretary to halt the tanks. The more problematic point is that if they really know what the General Secretary does or doesn't know, then someone should find out how they are doing it. Maybe they have someone here inside the Kremlin, for example?"

Colonel Yevgeni paused, warily awaiting the Minister's reaction. I may have gone too far, he thought to himself, and now the Minister will pour his wrath upon my head.

The Minister's voice was heard again, this time loud and clear, sure and decisive.

"Nonsense. I don't agree with you, Colonel."

Yevgeni heard the Minister's receiver slamming down then the line went dead, and he replaced his own receiver on the cradle. Only then did Yevgeni notice, for the first time, that Gregory had been standing behind him the whole time, apparently listening with great interest to his conversation with the Minister of Defense.

Back in the Minister's office in the war room, the adjutant walked in.

"Mister Minister, I've stopped the distribution of the dispatch. No one else has received it besides you."

"Well done", the Minister replied curtly.

The red telephone rang, and the adjutant picked up the receiver. Svetlana was on the line.

"The General Secretary of the Party Vladimir Petrovich Yermolov wishes the Minister to come to him immediately for a briefing."

Before the adjutant even had time to hang up, the Minister addressed him.

"Are you sure that this false and fictitious dispatch has not reached anyone?"

"Yes, Mister Minister, one hundred percent. Minister, the Party General

Secretary requests that you come to him urgently for a briefing."

The Minister of Defense nodded, got to his feet and left the room, his adjutant following, trying to keep up with his pace.

PARTY GENERAL SECRETARY VLADIMIR PETROVICH YERMOLOV turned to the head of the KGB, seated across from him.

"I understand that our Minister of Defense is incredibly busy now."

"Yes, Mister Secretary. He is mostly in Khamovniki, in General Staff Headquarters. Do you remember what I told you of the team that he put together and literally kept locked in the Intelligence Special Forces secret base?"

"Yes, I remember. They were later flown to Murmansk."

"Exactly. He hasn't been there for the past two days, but he still continues to speak to the team by phone. All this activity is still not clear to us, but very soon, I believe, we'll know precisely what they are doing there. By the way, that Colonel Nazarbayev, the Kazakh, is the only one of the secret gang who stayed in Murmansk. It turns out that he was aboard that trawler that was sunk in the North Sea."

"What?" the General Secretary replied, puzzled. "He was on the boat that was sunk by the British and the Americans?"

"Yes, Mister Secretary. But actually, it wasn't them that sank it ..." "What are you saying? Are you trying to confuse me? I still can't understand what they're plotting behind my back. So tell me again, this

Kazakh of Budarenko's, was he or wasn't he on the ship?"

"Sir, we have indications that the trawler was probably sunk by our own submarine."

"I don't believe this. Why would we do something like this?"

"I still don't have an answer to give you, but there are

too many question marks accumulating on that subject: the Minister's secret team, their stay in Murmansk, the presence of the Kazakh Colonel on the trawler that wasn't very far from where the American missile exploded, and now this thing with the submarine. Maybe someone here, on our side, wanted to silence the Kazakh Colonel for good. Now these are more than just suspicions, and we are trying very hard to connect all of the pieces in the puzzle. I promise you, Mister Secretary, that this will be done as quickly as possible."

The Party Secretary removed his glasses and placed them on the desk. He massaged his face with his fingers for some time, then finally spoke.

"My friend Mister KGB Director, I don't like, in fact I really dislike, what is happening around me, or to be more precise, behind my back. This is no longer a hunch, as I already know that I'm not being told the whole truth. I don't know who I can trust and who I should suspect, and all this just a few hours before we start a war with NATO and the Americans. This is an insane situation, truly insane. I hope that you understand that I need you closer to me than ever. Do you understand this?"

"Yes, Mister Secretary. Not only do I understand, but I'm working around the clock to protect you, and also to get you the maximum amount of information. As I told you before, we are very near to deciphering all those unknowns."

The Minister did not move his gaze from the Head of the KGB.

"I trust you. Don't disappoint me."

The Head of the KGB could have sworn that he could almost detect a plea in the eyes of the almighty General Secretary when he said "Don't disappoint me".

Svetlana entered the room and the Secretary looked at her in anticipation.

"Gospodin Vladimir Petrovich Yermolov, the Minister of Defense will arrive in three to four minutes."

The General Secretary turned to the Head of the KGB.

"You'd better go before he comes in, but stay close. I have a feeling that I'll be calling you back here today."

The two shook hands, and the Head of the KGB hurried out of the room.

The Minister of Defense, Marshal Budarenko, sat himself in the chair that the Head of the KGB had vacated just a few minutes before. The Party General Secretary could not miss the Minister's high spirits.

"How are our forces advancing in the field? Do we already have contact with the insurgents there?"

"Mister Secretary, we are even ahead of schedule. I'm pushing them to advance as fast as possible so that the enemy won't have time to mobilize. There's no civil resistance, and certainly no military resistance. Our main forces are not entering the cities of the German Democratic Republic at all. All of them are advancing to the real thing, leaving only small forces near several cities."

"So I understand that you are very content", the General Secretary said, not revealing any emotion.

"This is true, Mister Secretary."

The General Secretary did not move his gaze from the minister's face. "Especially since this is exactly what you've been planning all along, and you're not really interested in the civil disobedience and the

German Democratic Republic, are you?"

The Minister's smile froze in an instant, and he was as

tightly wound as a spring.

"Mister Secretary, that is not true. The difference between us is that I am a military man and I know that one should always prepare for any eventuality. What did you want? Did you want me to enter the Democratic Republic with limited forces? Then, if the Americans reacted by threatening us with military action and issuing us with an ultimatum, what would you have told them? Comrades, please wait a minute. I'm not ready. Give me few days to move several more divisions from the rear. That's how a civilian thinks, not a responsible military man."

By now the General Secretary's eyes were burning with rage.

"Meanwhile, the person running this country is the civilian before you, not the military man before me."

The Minister of Defense chose not to reply. The General Secretary, who was incandescent with anger, removed his glasses and cleaned the lenses with a cloth handkerchief in slow, circular motions, as though trying to control his emotions.

"And what do you have to say about the American President's speech today?" the General Secretary asked the Minister.

"Mister Secretary, I don't buy this garbage. I ran the subject by the Commander of our Air Force and all our intelligence agencies. He's trying to pull the wool over our eyes. I told you at our last meeting that no pilot can arm a nuclear warhead on a cruise missile by himself, even if he really wants to. This can only be done with special approval from supreme headquarters that sends a very specific code, just as we do. Regarding the coincidence, etc., it's only a one in a billion chance. In my opinion, the Americans are panicking in the face of our military might which is advancing toward their lines of defense as we speak, and this is all they have left to do. Namely, to implore, to ask for forgiveness, and to do with the Americans know best – offer us money, compensation. I hope you don't accept their apology."

The General Secretary ignored the Minister's suggestion and continued to rain questions on him.

"So you say that we're ahead of schedule. When are we going to cross the border between the Germanys and start the fighting?"

"Within 24 hours, maybe even less."

"If so, I would like to meet with our soldiers before that. When will that be possible?"

"I'm flying there tomorrow morning. I'll be happy if you come with me."

"All right. Keep me updated on any development until then, even if you think that it's negligible. Am I sufficiently clear?"

"You are clear, Mister Secretary. We'll meet tomorrow morning."

UNITED STATES PRESIDENT JAMES BUTLER OPENED THE third meeting of the day in the Situation Room, with his senior national security staff, advisors, and the Secretary of State. Two and a half hours had passed since he had faced the nation and reported the near- catastrophe that had allegedly caused the mistaken launch of a cruise missile armed with a nuclear warhead. The President's creatively ambitious plan seemed to have failed miserably. Worse, reports of the Soviet tank columns advancing more rapidly than expected added to the tense atmosphere, with a feeling that time was running out. There was a pall of despair over the Situation Room. It seemed obvious to everyone that war would break out within hours.

President Butler glanced quickly at the people around the conference table.

"Where is the CIA director? Why isn't he here?"

"Mister President, he'll be right here. He said that an important dispatch had just come in and he'll be here soon to brief you", the White House Chief of Staff replied quickly.

"Secretary Manning, please start."

"Mister President, it's strange, but we haven't heard back from them about your speech. This isn't like them at all. We even expected them to respond with disdain, but strangely enough, we've received no response at all. It appears that they are simply determined to move their tanks as rapidly as possible. What is stranger yet, Mister President, is that it appears that your directive ordering the conditional use of nuclear tactical weapons hasn't been intercepted by them at all. That is highly improbable."

"Maybe that's exactly what happened. It's hard to believe that anyone would remain indifferent to such an order that is signed by me."

"Mister President, the directive was distributed on dozens of networks. It would be impossible for them not to intercept and decipher it. It seems more likely that someone there decided that it was false. Maybe because it went through so many networks, their assessment is that this is a bogus threat. Mister President, even the method of their invasion and advance in East Germany indicates that the insurgency there was just an excuse, a cover story for their attack on us. Their forces haven't entered any city; they are simply racing to the West German border."

"Go on, Secretary."

"They are advancing in three columns. We identified their northern column as the primary force, and we assess that it's heading for Hamburg. This is one of the largest and most important Western European cities, but what seems to be of special interest to them there is the port. If they occupy the port of Hamburg, they will gain incredible abilities for pushing supplies and materiel to their forces."

The President listened, deep in thought. He smoothed his hair with his palm and watched the others.

"They will also export from Hamburg port – not just import", the President said.

Secretary Manning seemed to miss the point that the President was trying to make.

"Excuse me, Mister President, what do you mean?"

"They will do exactly what they did in World War Two. They'll take apart the entire West German heavy industry, load it onto trains and ships and transfer the plants and production lines to Russia. Okay, this isn't the time to discuss what they will do after conquering West Germany, when we don't even know what to do now. Secretary Manning, I understand that they are advancing much more rapidly than we estimated a few hours ago. What are your people saying now? How many hours do we have until they cross the border into West Germany?"

"Between sixteen and eighteen hours, Mister President."

"Great!" the President said sarcastically. "Maybe by then we'll have held seven or eight meetings like these, with no direction and purpose."

Nobody spoke, as the President's desperation reflected what all the others were feeling.

The door opened and CIA Director George Brown hurried in. The President looked at him, hoping that he was bringing some new information that could lift the heavy atmosphere in the room.

"Well", the President said in a tone lacking optimism. "Maybe, by chance, you have better news, or even a reason to give us hope?"

"Mister President, I have very substantial news that will clarify the picture, although I'm not sure it will change the situation."

"Go on, go on", the President said impatiently.

"Mister President, do you remember that there was a report of a single survivor from the Russian trawler, whom the British captured and transferred to us for interrogation?"

"Of course I do."

"It turns out that the fisherman that we caught is nothing less than a nuclear fisherman. He's a Red Army Colonel, born in Kazakhstan, and his name is Nazarbayev."

President Butler was jotting down the Soviet Colonel's name on a sheet of paper. The CIA director watched him, waiting to continue.

"Go on, go on", the President said.

"This Colonel is an explosives expert. He's a tough guy and he didn't cooperate until he was told, and believed, that a Soviet submarine had sunk his ship and his comrades, and only after we promised him political asylum. It turns out that aboard the trawler, they had a 152- millimeter self-propelled gun, and this gun fired a nuclear shell with a magnitude of one hundred kilotons."

"What?" the President interrupted. "What did they hope to gain by that?"

"Their operatives here in Washington got their hands on the training program of our assault nuclear submarines. At the time that they fired the shell, our submarine USS 726, the Ohio, should have been right there, underwater. Their idea was to set off the explosion after the Ohio had passed them and was further away, to make the commander of the Ohio believe that a much larger blast had occurred much farther away, meaning here on United States soil. The trawler was also equipped with electronic gear to block all communications from the submarine. They hoped that the Ohio commander would assume that a nuclear attack had been carried out on American soil and that that was why he couldn't establish communication with home.

"In their estimation, the submarine commander would have given the order to launch two or three nuclear missiles at predetermined targets in the Soviet Union, in accordance with the submarine's emergency procedure.

"What happened in fact was that a short time before the submarine was due to reach that area, it received an order to abandon the navigation exercise because of the DEFCON 2 alert, so it headed south. The enemy on the trawler was not aware of this, of course, and they fired the shell when the Ohio was already outside their range."

"And why would they do that?" the President asked.

"All this lunacy was created by their Minister of Defense, one Marshal Budarenko. Two weeks ago, he appointed a top secret special team, which included six senior experts in different subjects, and the Colonel that we caught was one of them. The Minister of Defense met this team almost daily at some top-secret military intelligence base outside Moscow."

The room fell into absolute silence. Butler shook his head

in disbelief.

"That man is a mental case. He is a lunatic and a loose cannon. Is he really willing to sacrifice millions of his people just for an excuse to invade Western Europe and save the Communist regime in the Soviet Union? I simply find it very hard to believe. This is beyond imagination. This is pure madness by a totally deranged individual", the President said.

The President watched Secretary of Defense Manning, who seemed utterly shocked.

"Of course", the President continued,"Party General Secretary Yermolov must not have the slightest idea of what this lunatic Minister is conspiring behind his back. Does he?"

"Of course not, Mister President", the CIA director replied. "The General Secretary is even certain that we tried to destroy the city of Murmansk. There's something else, Mister President. The source that we activated, with your approval, confirms unequivocally that General Secretary Yermolov has not an inkling of this whole affair."

President Butler breathed a huge sigh of relief, which sounded like a whistle.

"I made a big mistake, a rookie's mistake. I went ahead with my speech and played into the hands of this madman. Had I denied any connection with the blast and said that it was a Russian conspiracy, maybe the Party General Secretary would have started suspecting his Minister of Defense. I certainly made a major blunder with my address to the nation."

The Secretary of State turned to the President, requesting to speak.

"Mister President, when you made that speech, you didn't know if the Party General Secretary had any idea of what had really happened in the North Sea. Now the question is different. We know exactly who did what and why. How can it help us stop the tanks that are almost on our doorstep? Mister President, what if we display this Russian Colonel on television, so that the Russians can also see him and listen to what he has to say?"

President Butler took a moment to think before replying to his Secretary of State. The Situation Room was silent as every move and motion of the President was followed tensely by all the participants. They all waited eagerly for his decision. The President leaned forward, set his elbows on the table, and turned to the CIA director.

"How long will it take you to bring us one of your men who speaks Russian?"

"Right now, actually. I have a team working right outside this room and there is a fellow there who speaks fluent Russian. He was born here to a family who emigrated from the Soviet Union."

The President took up the phone receiver and handed it to the CIA director.

"Tell them to get this guy here at once. By the way, Secretary Perry, your TV idea isn't bad, but I want to take it even further."

Two minutes later, a tall Russian-looking young man stood at the door. He had a round face and fair skin and his hair was cut short. He seemed extremely nervous to be standing face-to-face with the President of the United States.

"What's your name?"

"My name is Vitaly Khripkin, Mister President." "Come here, Vitaly. Sit next to me."

The young CIA agent almost stumbled as we walked toward the President and took a seat beside him. The President put a fatherly arm on Vitaly's shoulder as he spoke to CIA director.

"Say, are you sure he's one of us? He looks like a classic KGB agent."

Khripkin moved uneasily in his chair, the President's arm still on his shoulder.

"I'm only kidding, son. Now listen up. I am about to make a phone call to the Soviet leader Yermolov. He doesn't speak English, and someone will have to translate what I'm saying. There's quite a bit of mayhem in the Kremlin right now. I don't know if whoever is translating for him has his own agenda, if he is loyal to Yermolov or maybe to his Minister of Defense. He may falsify my words. I would like you, Vitaly, to listen to the conversation on the extension and signal to me if everything is translated as should be. Do you understand me, son?

"Yes, Mister President, of course."

The President lifted the receiver of the telephone next to him.

"This is the President speaking. Please connect me to Moscow. I would like to speak to the General Secretary of the Party. This is extremely urgent."

The President, whose mood had started to improve in the past few minutes, now revealed his sense of humor, which was very much a defining trait in normal times. Holding the receiver to his ear, he spoke to his team around the table.

"You see, there are also advantages in the Soviet Union. I told the operator to get me the General Secretary of the Party in Moscow, and she did not have to ask me of which party."

Several nervous laughs sounded around the room. The President raised his hand and there was silence.

"Mister President Butler. This is Svetlana, personal secretary to Party General Secretary Sir Vladimir Petrovich Yermolov. The Party General Secretary will enter the room very soon, and I will act as your simultaneous translator from English to Russian and from Russian to English. So there is no need, Mister President, to take pauses as you speak."

"Very well, Ma'am. Thank you."

The President continued to hold the line for his Soviet counterpart. He covered the mouthpiece with his hand and whispered to the CIA director.

"Listen, she works in a strategic place and also has wonderful English. Why don't you guys recruit her? Do I need to give you ideas?"

The American spy chief smiled reservedly.

"Only a few hours ago I did offer you, Mister President, a job at our agency as your post-Presidential career."

Svetlana came back on the line, and the President motioned Vitaly to pick up the extension.

"Here you are, Sir, President Butler."

"*Dobriy vecher*, Mr. General Secretary Yermolov", President Butler greeted his Soviet counterpart with a "good evening" in Russian. "I would have liked to speak to you under much happier circumstances, but it seems that there is someone on your side who prefers that we speak with our rifles."

President Butler heard Svetlana translating his words and took a look at Vitaly at his side, who nodded to him in confirmation that his words were being correctly translated. Now the Party General Secretary's voice was heard in the background, with Svetlana translating his words.

"The Party Secretary asks if this is the best opening you could find for your mutual conversation?"

"I am sorry then, Mister Secretary. I know you are an honorable man, and if you'll please just listen to me for three minutes, I'm sure that we will succeed together in preventing a third World War."

"The Party Secretary is listening to you, Mister President."

"Mister Secretary, we did not launch any missile in the North Sea and we have nothing to do with the nuclear blast. Your trawler was sunk by your own submarine. What your people do not know yet is that one person aboard the trawler survived, and his name is Colonel Nazarbayev. He told us about a secret team that was put together by your Minister of Defense, Marshal Budarenko. I can give you all the details of the Intelligence base in Moscow, where this Colonel and five other senior officers worked in isolation and in secrecy for the Minister of Defense. I can tell you how many times your Minister of Defense has visited this team in the past ten days. This Colonel Nazarbayev is the person who fired a nuclear artillery shell from a gun which they loaded onto the trawler at the Naval Base in Murmansk. Their mission was to create the explosion close to one of our nuclear submarines in order to simulate a much larger nuclear attack on the United States. All this just so the submarine commander would reach the mistaken conclusion that our mainland had been attacked, causing our submarine to launch a nuclear missile in response at the Soviet Union.

"Mister Secretary Yermolov. Can you see that your Minister is ready to sacrifice millions of your civilians just so he can have his excuse to flood Western Europe with thirty thousand of your tanks? Mister Secretary, allow me to voice my opinion of this man. I think he is insane and very dangerous. If you don't stop him, we will be in a state of total war by morning. Does Mister Secretary know that I've issued an order to destroy your tanks with tactical nuclear weapons if they cross the Elbe River? Is Mister Secretary aware of this, or maybe this too was concealed from you by your Minister of…?"

The President paused at a gesture from Vitaly, who put his hand over his receiver and whispered to the President:

"Something is not right with her."

"What do you mean?" the President asked.

"Sir, she is translating everything verbatim, but something in her voice has changed. I think she's choking, or maybe she's crying. It's not clear." Svetlana's voice was heard again.

"Please hold, Mister President."

Vitaly made a huge effort to get something of the conversation on the other end, which sounded too weak and far away to make out. He raised the volume on his phone and closed his eyes, trying to concentrate on the conversation as much as possible. The President followed him with great interest, as did everyone else in the room.

"Mister President, this is unbelievable. She is crying and the Party Secretary is telling her that he's sorry that she had to hear all this from the President of the United States and not from him. I couldn't hear everything, but I heard the Secretary say something like it's your uncle, if am not mistaken." Svetlana's voice was heard again.

"Mister President Butler. The party Secretary Mister Vladimir Petrovich Yermolov thanks you for calling him. He says that he is willing to stop all our forces where they are at 10 o'clock Greenwich Mean Time tonight. At the same time exactly, you shall cancel the supreme alert to all your forces, on land, sea and air."

The President extended his hand forward and made the thumbs up signal to his Secretary of Defense, who responded with a nod of his head.

"I know the General Secretary is a man of honor", President

Butler said to Svetlana, "and I accept his proposal. I give you my word, and so it will be. I will be delighted to speak to him again tomorrow. Thank you, Ma'am, and good night."

"Good night, Mister President."

The President got to his feet, thanked Vitaly and shook his hand, and addressed his Minister of Defense.

"Secretary Manning, you heard the agreement we have reached with the Leader of the Soviet Union, right? At 22:00 hours Greenwich Mean Time you de-escalate our forces to DEFCON 3. Activate all our Intelligence sources to ensure that all Soviet forces in East Germany will indeed be ordered to stop where they are and that they obey this order."

THE HEAD OF THE KGB HURRIED INTO THE OFFICE OF THE PARTY GENERAL SECRETARY. Displaying his pride in their friendship, the General Secretary rose up, walked around his large desk and took a seat next to the head of the KGB.

"Thank you for arriving so quickly."

"Mister Secretary, you did ask me to remain close by today, and that's exactly what I've done. Unfortunately, Sir, I have news that you may not like, and it all has to do with Marshal Budarenko's activity."

The Party Secretary nodded. He looked resigned.

"Nothing you say can surprise me anymore. I've just finished speaking with United States President. They caught one survivor from the trawler, and the survivor is Colonel Nazarbayev. The Colonel understood that he had been betrayed and he told them everything – everything. He told them of his meetings with the Minister, the plan, the nuclear shell that he himself fired from the trawler. He told them everything.

"You understand that this deranged Marshal Budarenko wanted the Americans to fire nuclear missiles at us from their submarine just so he could have a reason to conquer half the world with his tanks? Do you understand in what hands our national security rests? Now listen to my orders. I command you to arrest the Minister of Defense immediately, and all his team of aides and advisers – the whole gang. Arrest the Commander of the Navy, the Commander of the Naval Base in Murmansk and the Commander of the Air Force. I want all of them in jail tonight. Each and every single one of them! Also, arrest the traitors from his secret team."

The General Secretary's voice grew louder and louder, and his face reddened as he spoke.

"First of all, I want them all in jail, and then they can try to prove their innocence. If you know of any other rogue criminals, arrest them too. You don't need my preapproval. Do what needs to be done and do it quickly."

The General Secretary leaned back in his chair and lit a cigarette, something he didn't do very often.

"I really don't know who I can consult with from among the Politburo members. Who can I trust and who should I mistrust? This is absurd. What the hell am I going to do with the military? At exactly 10 o'clock Greenwich Mean Time I'm stopping all the forces in their tracks. But what should I do with them? If I bring them back home, they might rise against me because I threw their greatly beloved and admired Marshal into jail. On the other hand, if they stay so close to the German border, the Americans will think that I'm toying with them, and every little skirmish there on the border might develop into total war."

The head of the KGB, who had so far listened intently to

the General Secretary, sat up in his chair.

"Mister Secretary, perhaps you should fly to the front and meet with the commanders there, and brief them about the Minister of Defense's conspiracy. I will come with you."

"I think you're right. I'll fly there tomorrow morning, but you – I need you here. You will have your hands full. You'll have to guard the Motherland until I return."

The head of the KGB solemnly placed his hand on his chest and looked directly into the eyes of the General Secretary.

"Go in peace and return in peace, Mister Secretary. I am responsible for everything here running as it should."

The Party General Secretary remained in his large office by himself. He lit another cigarette and savored every puff. Tomorrow I will stand before all the commanders of the Soviet Armed Forces; the commanders of the armies, divisions and maybe even brigades, he thought to himself. I'll either be buried over there, or I will return as the supreme, undisputed leader of this great nation of the Soviet States.

The great hangar in a German Democratic Republic Air Force base was packed with the top echelons of the Red Army. The hundreds of officers sat on their chairs in suspense. Just a few hours ago, they had received the order to stop where they were, and now they had been summoned for an unscheduled meeting with their supreme leader, the General Secretary of the Communist Party, the most powerful man in the Soviet Union.

The feeling among many of the participants was that the Secretary had come to give them his personal blessing directly before they climbed into their tanks and crossed the border into West Germany.

They all rose to attention as the General Secretary entered the hall and stepped up the stage and then, without preamble, he began recounting the story of their former Minister of Defense, Marshal Budarenko, to his stunned audience; of his conspiracy and betrayal against himself, against the Armed Forces and against the Soviet nation. The General Secretary gave the officers details of the former minister's actions, and also informed them of the arrests that had been made the previous night and those that were still being made as he spoke.

A hum of whispers was heard from the crowd of officers. The Secretary silenced them with a motion of his hand.

"I have come here to you to hear your decision. Do you wish to fight a World War, or do you wish to go back home to the Motherland and to your families? It is from you that a new leadership will rise for our great Red Army. It is from you that a reliable and loyal leadership will rise for the Motherland and for Socialism."

The Secretary ended his speech and watched the officers in the hall, who had fallen into complete silence. The officers sneaked looks around them, and closely examined the reactions of their more senior officers, who were seated in the first rows.

Then all of a sudden, an Army commander, a Major General, rose to his feet in the first row. The officers looked at him in anticipation.

"Long live Comrade General Secretary Vladimir Petrovich Yermolov, Leader of the Soviet Union!" the Army commander called out in a thundering voice.

Within seconds, the whole hangar was shaking with cries of: "Hurray! Hurray! Hurray!"

The General Secretary remained standing on the stage,

finally allowing himself a broad smile, for the first time in many days.

Three days earlier

It was late at night when Svetlana, the General Secretary's private secretary, retired to her home after a day's work. She wanted to relax and catch up on her sleep, which had been so lacking in the past few days.

Someone knocked on her door. Svetlana looked through the peephole and there stood a young man in uniform. He held a bouquet of flowers.

Svetlana felt as if she were about to faint. Her hand shook as she opened the door, gave the messenger a 10-ruble note, took the bouquet quickly, and locked the door behind her. She stood there for a long moment, leaning against the door, while her hands, still holding the bouquet of flowers, shook violently. She was obviously shocked.

The bouquet was quite an unusual one, containing a mix of flowers of different types and colors. She walked to the dining room table and placed the flowers there, then sat down in a chair.

Her hands still shaking, she began taking the bouquet apart and separating the flowers, one by one, by colors and types. The table was now completely covered with flowers of different groups. She counted the flowers one by one according to their types and quickly jotted down letters and numbers on a sheet of paper.

I should have known this moment would arrive, she murmured to herself. There was no way the Americans would leave me be when the world's two superpowers are on the brink of war.

EPILOGUE

Moscow, May 1989

The father and son had now been sitting for more than two hours in a corner of the famous Pushkin Café. This was a well-known establishment, famous throughout the world, and not just for its excellent coffee, dark wood interior and book-laden shelves. The place was also an outstanding restaurant, adjacent to Pushkinskaya Square, bearing the name of Russia's greatest poet. At the center of that square, a tall dark grey marble column bore the bronze statue of the poet Alexander Sergeyevich Pushkin, towering over its surroundings.

The former head of the KGB sipped the rest of his hot chocolate and then looked at his son's face. "Did you understand, my son? I had the great honor of serving General Secretary Yermolov, and I helped him to prevent a third world war at the last minute. This would have been the most unnecessary war, just thirty-six years after the Soviet nation sacrificed twenty-two million soldiers and civilians in the Great Patriotic War."

The son could hardly tear his gaze from his father.

"Father, this is the first time I have heard you speak of that sad affair."

The former Head of the KGB combed his thinning hair with his fingers and smiled lightly.

"Yes, son, and at my advanced age, it is also the last time."

THE END

43067370R00139

Made in the USA
Middletown, DE
19 April 2019